House of Shadows

SECRETS NEVER DIE

Christian Mystery Romance

Crystal Mary Lindsey

Award Winning Author

Retired

Registered Nurse B.S.N.

Professional Counselor

Bible College Graduate

BIBLE VERSE

For, "THE ONE WHO DESIRES LIFE,

TO LOVE AND SEE GOOD DAYS,

MUST KEEP HIS TONGUE FROM EVIL

AND HIS LIPS FROM SPEAKING DECEIT."

1 Peter 3:10

To

Father

Son

And

Holy Spirit

Chapters

Chapter 1

June 1902 New Orleans

Applause pulsated from the standing audience. Smiling faces shone in admiration of Mariah Kingsford's glorious voice as she stood center stage, spotlighted. She looked poised and composed yet felt neither.

Exhaustion was all she perceived, no jubilation as the admirers expected, her smile was a forced mask as were her waist bending bows of appreciation.

"More, more," shouts began from the frenzied crowd as the clapping escalated.

Mariah's voice overjoyed her fans, and they wanted it to continue.

Did she have one more song to provide? She had given two extra encores. NO, there was to be no more.

It had been difficult getting through the two-hour performance. Every song put behind her drew her closer to the conclusion. Thankfully now she was done, finished. With one last curtsy and smile, and blowing a kiss, she walked elegantly from the stage.

"Mariah, give them another song," her manager Jake tried to persuade as she walked by him. His balding head shone with sweat as he mopped it with his handkerchief. He ran alongside his star trying to keep up with her fast pace.

Why was he sweating when I did all the work, she glared at him with distaste on the lovely tired face?

The French Opera House, in New Orleans, unbeknown to them, had seen the last of the Golden Lark. It was vacation time but more than that, she was going home, she needed rest, and no one was going to get around her this time.

It was years since she'd seen the family plantation home. As a young girl, she couldn't wait to leave and venture out into the world.

Coming to New Orleans and traversing for beautiful clothes in the many colorful bouquets was a welcoming world. One that she made the best of, learning to dress exquisitely.

Procure a job singing in the chorus of The French Opera House in New Orleans, was unbelievable. Mariah was coached in diction and applied Italian language instruction.   Within her first year, she rose to become the understudy to Georgette Leblanc.

 The flurry of parties, social and political events followed with Mariah meeting the full cross-cultural setting of New Orleans society.

By 1898 Mariah Grace Kingsford graduated to Mezzo-Soprano and Prima Donna when Madame Leblanc left America to returned to Paris.

Now ten years later from when Mariah left her heritage in North Carolina she was returning to where she truly belonged.

She pushed carefully passed the many well-wishers, her fellow singers in the troupe while being kissed or touched with the excitement of a successful performance. Mariah smiled weakly, only wanting to get to her dressing room, relax and be herself.

Opening the door and greeted by her companion maid Fay, Mariah stood looking down at the vases of flowers spread over the floor. Closing her eyes for a moment, then spinning around she looked down the hallway for Guy, the doorman.

Being hailed, Guy rushed to her side. "How are you, Mariah? You look tired out my little one."

Tears sprung momentarily to her eyes touched by his words of kindness. Mariah nodded in agreement.

"I have a favor to ask of you, please get these flowers out of here Guy, put them somewhere unseen for now. I can't handle the mixtures of scent. Tomorrow take them to the Nursing Home down the road please."

He could see she meant business and stood scratching his head. "All of them Miss, don't you want to keep the one from your manager and Sir Thomas?"

Striving not to get distressed as it wasn't Guy's fault, Mariah repeated, "Yes Guy all of them, and I mean that."

He quickly began to take out the ones immediately in her way of entry, lining them against the outside wall. "I'll clear these off first and then come back for the rest." Looking at her and hoping she'd be happy with that, he was glad of her weak smile.

"Thank you, Guy, and take whichever ones you like home to your wife." He doffed his cap. "Thank you, Miss. Kingsford; she will appreciate that."

Mariah headed straight to her dressing table and sat down, leaning her arms on the top to support her face while kicking off her shoes.

"Thank God tonight is over Fay, if you'd told me ten years ago that I'd burn out from traveling the world and singing for my keep, I'd have laughed. "

"Are you that weary of it Mariah?" Fay looked concerned at the employer she adored. In her mid-thirties, Fay Gates had been with Mariah since shortly after the singer's arrival in New Orleans with her parents. Without a job, Mariah's mother quickly hired Fay as a chaperone and maid to her daughter, then sixteen-years-old.

Mariah sat staring at herself in the mirror noting the weariness especially visible around her eyes. "Yes I am extremely tired Fay, as you know, we have barely had a decent vacation in the last eight years. I know you must have felt the stain as well."

"I'm just thankful for having a good job and all the traveling I've been able to do. God has taken care of us, and it's exciting."

Mariah looked at her in the mirror, marveling as always at Fay's sweet disposition. Fay was a person small of the statue with large gray eyes and dark brown hair. She had the most beautiful smile that showed her perfect teeth. Why she'd never married was a mystery and one she refused to discuss.

"Let's have a cup of tea together Fay please and lock that door; I don't want anyone to enter until I've had time to catch my breath."

"And Guy?"

"Oh yes, of course, I forgot about him. See if he's on his way back and perhaps you might help him to get the rest of these flowers out. Then lock the door."

Mariah began to clean the heavy make-up off her face. Her skin looked healthy, and her blue eyes shone beneath the natural dark lashes, her lips were full and attracted many a second glance from interested males. The dimple in her cheek looked of innocence and a delight in life.

Remove the pins from her blond hair and allowing it to topple loosely down past her shoulders, her slender fingers stretched out to massaged her scalp. Mariah glanced in the mirror now and then watching Guy and Fay wandering in and out, dispensing with the floral arrangements.

When all were gone, Fay turned to close and lock the door? Her attempt was interrupted by a foot shoved in the doorway to prevent closure. Sir Thomas Whittaker roughly pushed passed her without requesting permission and entered the room.

He was a tall man with dark brown hair and piercing hazel eyes. Being from English nobility, he considered himself above any boundaries or guidelines. Looking around the room and then at Mariah, he removed his hat and stood in disbelief, not seeing the large bouquet he'd sent.

"Did you get my floral arrangement?" With a frown on his face, he stared at her reflection in the mirror.

Mariah was tired of his demands and of him taking her for granted. Time, and again he was told that she was not going to answer to him. They were neither engaged nor related and were never likely to be.

Exasperated by his arrogance, she turned in her swivel chair and looked to her maid.

"Did we Fay?" She raised her eyebrows and yawned revealing her boredom.

His temper elevated as he demanded, "What do you mean, did we? The bouquet was massive, - and for you, not her! Didn't you read my note?"

Fay turned to make the tea without answering Mariah's question. She didn't know what to say, and this man made her anxious with his bullying ways. She was afraid of him.

Thomas turned to confront Fay, "Out now, I want to speak to your mistress alone." There was no waiting for a reply; he didn't want one. He flung open the door, and disrespectfully his arm encircled her waist to forcibly guiding her out. "Thank you," he slammed the door shut in her face.

Striding over to Mariah he seized her arm and roughly pulled her from the chair. "What's all this nonsense? Don't go trying to take me for a fool Miss. or you'll find yourself taking on more than you've bargained. Do I make myself clear!" His angry face thundered down at her with eyes flashing a dangerous warning.

Fay hadn't gone far; she was listening at the door, her hand rising to cover her mouth shocked by the violence she heard. Turning quickly on her heel, she ran down the hall and out of the stage door, into the alley with feet flying. Rounding the corner into Bourbon Street and sighting a police officer she hastened to tell him. Miss. Mariah was in trouble.

Everyone knew who Miss. Mariah was, and the policeman blew his whistle summoning backup. It didn't take long for two more officers to arrive. Briskly they followed Fay as she retreated through the Opera House stage door and on to Mariah's dressing room.

Standing outside of the star's room and listening to the loud noise from within one policeman instructed the other two. Thomas's voice rose, followed by a scream from Mariah and a loud thud on the floor that sent the officers into action. Throwing themselves against the locked door, they forced entry, with batons raised.

Mariah sat on the floor, silently weeping while Thomas stood menacingly over her. Fay ran to assist her friend while two of the officers apprehended the angry man assaulting her.

"You are in deep trouble Monsieur." The third officer

pointed a shaking finger. "Judge Leon does not take the use of force on the weaker sex lightly."

"Don't be too sure of that, because you will be the one in trouble yourselves when the Judge learns who I am," Thomas shouted in retaliation, shaking with anger.

Hands cuffed behind his back; he was led off while still trying to resist. The one officer remaining took out a notebook and sat to write his incident report. With a tired sigh, Mariah told him everything including her constant affirmation to Sir Thomas, that she was not interested in him.

"He just never takes any notice!" her shoulders shook as she cried into a handkerchief. Then suddenly realizing the repercussions, she asked with a startled. "Must I attend court? It would be such unpleasant publicity."

"No Madame," the police officer assured kindly. "You will not! And since its Friday your attacker will be kept in the lock-up until Monday. He will then appear before Judge Leon, and if he is still in the same temper as now, the good judge will not take it kindly."

Having written notes on what Mariah informed him, the Officer prepared to leave.

"You must not worry about this Mademoiselle; the Judge will be very angry to hear what happened to such a fine lady as yourself. We will take care of everything."

With a salute and bow, he took his leave, walking off with long strides.

Fay already had a cup of tea prepared for them both. Handing one to Mariah, she sat to have her's. "Are you alright dear one? Or should I go for a doctor?"

"No, I'm okay Fay, and thank you for acting so quickly, I hate to think what else he would have done." She sipped the hot tea while closing her eyes. She felt so weary, and now, battle wounded as well.

"Look, Fay, I'm not bothering with anything else here tonight, we are going home." She stood picking up her coat and put it on.

"Yes! You have had enough for today; I'll come back tomorrow and clean all this up." Fay collected her coat and followed Mariah out of the door.

Chapter 2

Calculated Plans

It was eleven next morning before Mariah awoke. Laying in bed, she rejoiced in the luxury of not having to hurry off anywhere for the day. Closing her eyes, she thanked God it was over, perhaps she'd feel differently in time and want to return to her career, but for now, she needed to allow herself time to rest and recuperate.

The apartment door slammed shut with Fay's return. Mariah heard her in the kitchen before footsteps came her way. With eyes closed, she spoke. "I'm awake my dear, but still feeling worn out and needing to rest. I don't know why I feel like this?"

"Well, I do," came the reply. "Now, if I bring you some tea and toast, will you eat?"

"Yes, I need to, please make it a poached egg on toast

instead, plus a pot of tea. Can you bring yours in here to eat with me?" Mariah sat up leaning back on the many cushions and closing her eyes once more.

Fay nodding in agreement. "Certainly, we can have a tray each."

Mariah drifted off again needing to be woken up to have her meal.

"You poor darling, here, let me fix these pillows and make it comfortable for you." Fay fussed over her with love. They were more like sisters than employer and employee. Since meeting Mariah, Fay devoted her life to be closer than a meer companion.

Many men tried to gain Fay's affections, and although Mariah insisted she have her own life, Fay remained by her side. "If Mr. Right ever comes along, I'll let you know." She laughingly informed her employer.

 With pillows to better support her, Mariah poured the hot tea and took a sip before remembering to say, Grace. Fay sat over from her and watched as Mariah spoke her prayer, then slowly began to eat.

"Well, where do we go from here Mariah, have you thought about it or will we talk another time?" Fay was delicately eating a piece of toast held between two fingers and dipped into the egg yolk.

She waited for a response that was slow in coming. Pouring her tea, adding sugar and milk Fay wondered if Mariah could decide their next step or whether she might be the one to sort it out. Things didn't seem bright.

Mariah was thinking; then her face took on a look of determination. Her mind had puzzled something out, and she was pleased with the result.

"I am figuring out a plan for us Fay, but it's one that we must be cautious about." Drinking the rest of her tea and placing the cup onto the saucer she sank back against her pillows.

"Although I am tired, we need to move quickly because Sir Thomas could be out on bail come Monday. He will probably head straight to this house looking for us. How I wish father were here to handle him because we can't."

"Yes, I'm sure he will be searching everywhere. Well, he'll find no signs at the Opera House, and neither will anyone else come Monday. If then." Fay smiled while looking secretive.

Mariah's eyes lit up cheekily. "So, what have you done my Fay?"

"Well, you said you didn't like most of the gowns except the white, blue and silver. So I kept them as well as the two black that you mentioned needing. I cleaned out the room and got rid of all that old stuff. But, I put it into that big old suitcase and left them there in case someone wants them. That's all, but there is nothing of us remaining."

These words brought a smile to Mariah's face; then she began to laugh. "Good," was said between breaths of laughter.

"Now - I have something else for you to do, I want you to go to the rail and purchase two first-class tickets for us to Atlanta, Georgia, to leave as early as possible tomorrow morning."

"Oh really…. Georgia," Fay gaped, "What's in Georgia?"

"Nothing my dear, but we go there first to put anyone who wants to follow us, off the track."

"OH,!" Fay's face lit up with revelation. "And, where from there?"

"Only for the moment that's for me to know Fay, but I do have it worked out, so don't worry."

She held her tray out for Fay to remove, then throwing back the bed covers she was up. "I have to visit the water closet, but I'll be right back."

The two women lived in a small section of the large home belonging to Mariah's parents who were off somewhere in Europe.

Elsie and Henry, the husband and wife housekeeper and odd jobs man, resided in a back portion of the house. Otherwise, all else was empty. However, from the outside no-one would know if they were inside or not. Mariah would see to that.

Fay gathered up the trays and dishes taking them back to the kitchen for Elsie to take care of later.

A chest sat on the floor, open and ready to pack with gowns to take with them.

Returning to the room, Mariah stopped beside the settee, immediately picking up some gowns and depositing them inside. The two black were left out; they were for tomorrow.

"While you are away, I am going to finish packing in here, and when you return, you can put yours in as well. I want to get it finished and closed to be sent to the railway station with Henry as soon as possible. That way it won't be connected to us moving."

Mariah dragged her tired body around getting done what was needed. Then went to her parents living quarters to find men's wear belonging to her father. On the second leg of their journey, Mariah intended to dress as a young man. Thankfully, although her father was tall, he was also slim. All she needed to do was to shorten trouser legs and coat arms, and they'd be right.

Boots were Mariah's only problem as her fathers feet were enormous.

Fay would need to go back to the Opera House and get a pair off Guy. She could swop him a pretty gown for his wife.

All done, Mariah walked into her bedroom and collapsed on the bed.

Fay found her there a few minutes later when returning from her errand. She burst into their rooms full of excitement. "I got them, first class and leaving at 7 am, so being Sunday people will either be in bed or getting prepared for church, either way, we should get away without much notice."

She picked up Mariah's receptacle and put the tickets safely inside, eyes shining. "And, the ticket clerk informed me, the train doesn't get many passengers at that time of morning."

"That's wonderful Fay; I pray it works out without incident." Mariah yawned. She hoped to get a little more sleep. "It must be getting on in time, but I need you to go out once more and please bring us each back a pastie to tide us over until supper."

She informed Fay of needing her size in men's boots from Guy, without telling him why. They would be in the costume department. In return, Fay was to give him the cutest gowns from the old case. Mariah could imagine his joy when presenting them to his wife, and her pleasure to receive them.

That night over supper Henry gave Mariah the ticket needed to retrieve her chest at their final destination. He knew it to be confidential, and neither he nor Elsie would betray the trust.

Mariah handed over six months wages to cover the pair until her parents returned.

"What I need you to do Elsie, is to light lamps in all the rooms every night and to put them out when you retire. Seeing this from the outside will fool anyone watching."

Mariah informed them of the trouble with Sir Thomas

Whittaker and that he may likely come calling.

"I hope not, but if he does then tell him, I am away for the moment. Should he cause a problem, then you need to inform the law without haste. " Henry and Else looked at each other hoping it didn't come to that.

Seeing their looks, Mariah continued. "Then again he may be locked up in jail for a time, I certainly hope so."

The husband and wife nodded in agreement; they hoped the same.

With hugs, Mariah and Fay said goodnight and goodbye as they left the kitchen. They were retiring early and taking a cab to the station first thing in the morning with only a suitcase each containing their immediate necessities for the next three days.

Early next morning saw two beautifully dress ladies boarding the train for Atlanta, Georgia. With no complications, it was smooth sailing. They were the only passengers seated in first-class accommodated, which served them well.

The guard wandered through taking tickets and asking if they required anything: Mariah request two pillows, one for each of them to recline and sleep if need be. With a salute, the guard went to fulfill the request. The ladies removed their hats to make themselves comfortable in the rocking carriage; once they were alone again after receiving their needs, they could relax back and close their eyes.

Mariah had no idea how long she slept but woke suddenly with a start. She had dreamt Sir Thomas was standing over her. Instead, it was the guard wondering whether to awaken her or not.

"Didn't mean to bother you, Miss., but we'll be stopping at another station in twenty minutes, and I'll be busy for a while at that time. Did you want lunch? If so there is a dining car, or I can bring something to you now." He wore a pleasant smile on his brown face and his eyes reflected his desire to please.

Mariah glanced over at Fay and seeing she slept decided not to bother this kindly man in looking after them; they could do it themselves.

"I'm sure you have plenty to do. So no thank you, we shall enjoy a walk to the dining car and will go shortly." She smiled up at him showing genuine appreciation for his service.

Watching him leave their saloon Mariah called softly to Fay, "Are you awake Fay?"

"Yes I am," she yawned. "I heard every word, and you made the right choice, it will be nice to get up and walk, plus see something of the rest of the train."

Pulling herself up to a sitting position and with a yawn, Fay looked out of the window. "Do you know where we are Mariah?"

Shaking her head, Mariah conveyed, "Well since the guard said we are coming into a town, I guess we'll find out then."

The ladies tidied one another's hair - as without a mirror the job was impossible. Replacing their hats, and looking presentable once more, Mariah led the way out of the saloon and through the next carriage. It was only half full with everyone appearing tired, some sleeping and others looking like they just woke up. Holding on to the seats and balancing with the sway of the train they made it to the dining car.

Thankfully again it was almost empty with only two table's occupied. When seated, each looked at the menu. Mariah raised an eyebrow, "it reads well doesn't it Fay, I didn't expect such a variety."

Fay smiled and looked down again. "Yes it does, I think I'd like a cheese and mushroom crepe with a croissant and a cup of tea."

Mariah considered this a good choice, so ordered the same for both, from the hovering waiter. "Would you like the tea served first Madame?" he inquired.

"Yes, that would be nice, Thank you."

The train was slowing, and both looked out of the window to see the name of the station. "Tus-cal-oosa, Fay sounded out the name. I have never heard of it, have you, Mariah?"

"No, I can't say that I have, but it looks remarkable. Look at the buildings, and there is a ladies college. The students are all dressed alike." She leaned against the window trying to look to the side. "Even this station is pretty Fay look at all the flower pots." Mariah's eyes wandered everywhere; there was much to see and not knowing how long they would remain stopped, she didn't want to miss any of it.

"There are a lot of people getting on the train too," Fay added. "Looks like we may be sharing our saloon."

"Hm, well, some of these people look snobby, I don't feel like sharing with ones who consider themselves to be above others."

"It's a good thing we were first to choose our seats, and with our cases and pillows minding them, there shouldn't be any problem." Fay winked.

The waiter arrived with a teapot, utensils, milk, and sugar. Placing them gracefully in front of each lady, he stood back with a slight bow and smile.

Both women returned his smile and thanked him before Fay took the lead to pour. Mariah gave him a tip which he surveyed in his hand before placing in his pocket. With a grateful nod, he walked away.

Chapter 3

A Spiritual Gift from God

Mariah and Fay ate with leisure enjoying their meal. There was no hurry they would be spending the night and most of the next day onboard the train. Neither minded, it was nice to take their time without having to rush.

Mariah decided she could now reveal what they'd do when reaching Atlanta.

"Fay, I was reluctant to tell you my plans before until I got it all worked out in my mind." She looked up, Fay watched and waited, knowing it to be different to what she would do. Mariah was adventurous and like drama.

"We'll get off the train at Atlanta, then book into the New Kimble House Hotel. Hopefully, no one will recognize us. It should be nice to stay and rest for two days before changing our appearances and taking the steamboat to Greensboro."

Catching on to their destination Fay exclaimed. "We are going to your old family home aren't we?" Fay eyes glowed with excitement. "I've heard so much about it so I can't wait to see for myself, you've been away for a long time haven't you Mariah."

Mariah's face took on a faraway look, "Yes, I was sixteen when I left with my parents, not long before we met you, dear Fay. My Aunt Milly lives there alone with a housekeeper and two dogs, a couple of goats and a cat." She smiled, "at least she did when I was there."

"Does your aunt know we are coming?" Fay couldn't remember posting a letter to Swansboro.

Mariah dabbed her mouth with a napkin; she'd finished eating and felt refreshed. "No she doesn't yet, Fay, I intend to send her a telegram from Greensboro. It's no use her having to wait days before we get there." She sat back in her seat waiting for her friend.

"You've hardly eaten a thing Mariah, can't you try to have some more."

"I've had enough, for now, perhaps tonight, I'll see."
She seemed to be dreaming; there was a faraway look in
her eyes.

Fay finished her food and pushed the plate away, "What
are you thinking about?" she questioned.

"Ahhh wait and taste the food at my aunt's. The fresh
fish, cornbread to die for and fried okra. There is none
other like it." Mariah sighed. "It's been too long Fay, but
I still remember how good it was."

Fay did not comment, then changed the subject. "Okay,
let's get back to our seats and see if we have new
companions." She drew closer to Mariah and whispered,
"what do we say if someone recognizes you."

"Hm, that's a thought, we'll just be evasive, we don't
need to answer to anyone." She took hold of Fay's arm,
as they walked back to their saloon, careful not to fall as
the carriages rocked from side to side.

Holding tightly to a seat occupied by a woman with two
young children, Mariah's eyes lit on the tight white face

of the little boy. Aged about seven his large eyes stared back.

Mariah smiled at him. "Have you had your meal yet," she inquired, thinking he would have.

"No!" he replied sadly. "Me muvver can't afford it."

"Tommy, that's enough," his mothers face flushed with embarrassment. "Leave the lady be!"

Mariah was stunned by this revelation and looked at Fay while wondering what she could do. Spotting the porter walking towards them, she touched Tommy on the head and walked past his seat. Arriving in front of the porter, Mariah extracted money from her bag and explained the need to feed this little family.

"Bring them plenty, so they have enough until dinner tonight. And reserve a table for five to eat at seven o'clock." With a look at the money and then at the woman and children, he nodded and hurried off.

"That makes me feel so sad Fay. Let's see what we can

find out about them at supper. They may need help."

Fay walked through the door of the saloon slightly in front of Mariah, so she was first to see their seats occupied. Looked around for their suitcases, these sat on the floor further down on the opposite side of the carriage. Plenty of places remained vacant so what was the reason for those two women to claim theirs?

Fay and Mariah looked at one another. Then at the two women in their seats.

Fay spoke her mind loudly with a huff, "Well I never! how rude!"

Mariah tightened her grip on Fay's arm. She believed God impressed upon her a revelation about the older woman, and it was one that needed consideration.

"Let it go, Fay, we can sit somewhere else, the older lady needs the sun coming in the through the window."

"Mariah, what makes you think that?" Her friend gave a strange stare.

"Don't worry I know that I know! I've had God speak to me at various times, yet even though it's been some time, I know it's him. My mother told me I have a gift that some people receive. God wants us to know not to be hard on this lady but to accept it's his Will in the matter. Now come, let's find a place on the other side of the carriage."

Mariah wandered further down, collecting her suitcase and a cushion on the way until she found a seat with a window where she and Fay could both look out. Fay followed without a word knowing Mariah would open up and explain more about this Gift when they were alone together.

*****

A handsome man sat directly behind the seats chosen, reading a newspaper. He looked up fleetingly catching Mariah eye and smiled. Her blue eyes locked onto his and seemed unable to detach. Finally, she pulled them away seating herself with her back to him while withdrawing her hat for comfort.

Hart Carson-Rigby stopped himself from reaching forward to caress her lovely hair. He had been taken aback by the way their eyes locked and held and now watched with interest as her hair gleamed with golden sun streaks. Closing his eyes, he imagined its feel as he slid it through his fingers.

Miranda dropped her head as she settled with her back to him. Her heart pounded like that of a young girl who was unused to have a handsome mans' appraisal. Lowering her eyes as Fay glanced her way, she needed to consider why she felt as she did, without her friend's scrutiny.

Why would a stranger unsettle her? She had been in contact with many good-looking men over the years, with none affecting her. She remembered his amazing eyes, light gray with black fringed lashes that highlighted the color. His hair was dark mahogany and skin lightly tanned, and he sported a well-manicured mustache.

Yes, come to think of it! He didn't have the usual short beard or long side-burns that most southern men wore. Perhaps he was a northerner she considered. *Stop that; she chided herself why think about a stranger you'll likely never see again.*

Reaching over to Fay and touching her arm for attention she began to tell her more about the plantation she called home.

"It's a large home with servant quarters. We remained living there with grandfather after my grandmother died. He was an angry, mean man to everyone except me; I don't know why he was like that?"

"Why do you think he was nicer to you Mariah?" Fay's question was meaningful.

"I don't know why exactly, but from a young age I loved to sing, and he would sit me on his knee and listen. It was his idea that I should take singing lessons, and you know the rest."

Fay considered this and probed to learn more. "How was he mean to your family members?"

Mariah looked sad as she recalled what she had witnessed, especially when directed at her father. "He was a man who liked acknowledgment for everything and never considered himself to make mistakes. Everyone around him was at fault, especially my father when he was at home. Grandfather took delight in goading him." By the look on Mariah's face, she was reliving those days very clearly.

"You know my father dealt with the buying and selling of tobacco, he was prominent and liked by the plantation owners as a fair dealer. My grandfather could see no right in my fathers business. If it hadn't been for leaving my aunt Milly alone to contend with him, my parents would have left Fairways. "

Looking earnestly at Fay for understanding Mariah concluded, "It's a long story Fay, but when you meet Aunt Milly, you will see the sweet person she is. My parents knew she would receive all the tongue lashing of her father if they left."

"But finally they did leave Mariah!"

"Yes, I was their excuse, my grandfather had suffered a stroke by then which took away his speech as well as mobility, so the house became peaceful. A manservant was employed to care for the old man, and only a few months after we left, he passed away in his sleep."

"My goodness Mariah, your poor parents, and what about your Aunt Milly, has she never married?"

"I believe my aunt was in love with someone once, but my grandfather did short work of that. Aunt Milly should have run off with him. Instead, she was terrified to go against her father's wishes. Anyhow she could still marry, we'll have to give her some help and confidence Fay."

At this Fay looked dismayed. "She may not want us coercing her. We'll see how the land lays once we get there dear one."

On the way to the dining car that evening Mariah and Fay stopped beside little Tommy's seat. "Hello," Mariah extended her hand to the mother, introducing them both.

Learning the mother's name was Sarah, and the tiny girl Rebbecca, Mariah informed her.

"I have ordered a table for five because I hoped you and the children would dine with us."

Sarah blushed painfully. "My children may need something, but I am fine."

"It's supper time, and we all need to eat, so please share with us, it's my treat, and we will love to be with you and the children."

It took a little persuasion, but eventually, Sarah gave in and stood up, ushering Tommy in front of her. Mariah took his little hand in her's, smiling down at him, before guiding the way unsteadily to the dining car.

Their reserved table waited, already prepared.

"This is very kind of you," Sarah sat down, seating the little girl next to her, then Fay sat beside them, while Tommy proudly sat next to Mariah.

Over the meal of fried chicken with potato and carrots, Sarah shared some of her sad story, concluding that she didn't know where she was going after they got off the train at Atlanta.

"I am hoping to get employment there; it's supposedly a big city so there should be work."

"What of the children?" Fay looked bewildered.

"Tommy is seven, so he will look after Rebbecca while I'm busy," Sarak spoke with resignation.

Mariah's heart almost stopped with grief at hearing this. It was unthinkable.

"I have a better idea, Sarah," she decided on the spare-of-the-moment. "You can come and work for us. There will be plenty of room for you and the children to live in, and you won't be separated."

Sarah frowned, "do you honestly need help or are you making room for me out of pity."

"Well both in a way," Mariah confessed.

Then leaning across the table, she spoke confidentially. "You are escaping a brutal marriage, and we don't wish discovery either. Now, three women and two children are different from how we are at present. If anyone comes looking for us, we may fool them."

Sarah's face lit up. It sounded an excellent plan. "Yes, but the children might give us all away."

Mariah looked at Fay who held her hands in the air. "Don't bring me into this plan!"

Looking at Sarah again Mariah added. "How about if we dress Rebecca as a boy? She is too small to give us away.

What was your father name?"

"It was Alex Rebel Yarman."

"Fine, we could call her Rebel until we reach our destination, hows that?" Seeing the questioning look on Sarah's face, she added. "We'll buy some clothes in Atlanta, then more in Greensboro, don't be concerned about the money, I'll pay."

Chapter 4

Acting out the PLAN

Both women slept soundly in their small two-bed compartment. The constant sway of the train helped, while the wheels sped on carrying them closer to their next stop, the city of Atlanta.

Morning dawned with rain, it pelted down striking the windows and fogging the insides. Mariah sat up in bed, rubbing at the glass to see out but no sooner was it clear that it fogged up once more. She flopped down in her warm bed; her wristwatch was reading seven fifteen; it was going to be a long day if unable to look out at the passing scenery.

Fay groaned and stretched. "Are you awake Mariah?"

"Yes Fay," she murmured, "But I think I'll sleep a little longer, it's raining and without being able to sightsee today, the hours will drag."

"Well, you sound positive, I must say!" Fay rolled onto her stomach, head sideways as she looked over at the younger woman. "This is nice, rocking along while laying in bed. How about we plan to get up at nine, we'll miss the crowd if we go late to eat breakfast?"

"I agree," Mariah spoke with her eyes closed; it didn't take her long to return to slumber.

They dressed in the same black dresses as the day before not wanting to draw attention to themselves. On the way to the dining car, Sarah and the children were gathered to join them. Little Tommy was so excited about being with Mariah and having a meal. There was plenty to talk about and to learn off each other.

Purchasing fruit, bread, and cheese to keep for lunch they arranged to meet in the dining car again at six that evening. Sarah looked positively worn out, so Mariah made it a point to ask the porter if there was a two-bed sleeping car available.

The two children were small enough to sleep in one bed, and Sarah could rest peacefully in the other.

The young mother was told this over supper that night; tears flooded her eyes. "God is looking out for us through you two ladies, how blessed we are."

*****

Morning dawned with a weak sun peeping through overcast clouds. Sarah looked much refreshed after a better night and Tommy was full of telling them about the funny bed that moved all night to make him sleep. He had them all laughing at his imagination, and he felt a big boy being able to keep the grown-ups attention.

Since there was only an hour before arriving at their destination Sarah and the children were taken back to first class to remain with their new friends. The porter pretended not to see but winked at Tommy in answer to his call.

Preparing to alight at Atlanta the handsome man sitting behind them got up to leave the train as well. He was tall and broad-shouldered, dressed in an expensive suit with a brimmed hat in place. Standing back, he politely waited for women and children to go before him. Watching Sarah attempting to hold Rebbecca and also pick up a large bag, he reached forward helping with her suitcase.

"Where would you like this Mam?" Not wanting to place it onto the platform for her to struggle again, he took the cue off Mariah to carry and put it into a waiting cab. He lifted Tommy in making sure they settled before offering his name.

"Hart Carson is the name and pleased to be of service."

"Many thanks, Mr. Carson," Mariah answered without introductions. She felt there was no need giving away who they were when it could go against them at a later time.

He stood and watched as the carriage pulled away, suspecting these ladies were covering their tracks for some unknown reason. Taking out and lighting a cigar a mischievous smile curved his lips. *"We'll meet again sweet lady; I'm not so easily put off*. HM, Mariah was it? I might not know your last name, but I heard your Christian one spoken."

*****

The lobby of the new Kimble House Hotel resembled a metropolis bustling with activity. Mariah hadn't counted on this, but they weren't going anywhere else. Leaving Fay, Sarah and the children sitting on a lounge watching the comings and goings, Mariah approached the desk for service.

The male hotel clerk looked up from gathering papers and stared. A smile lit up his face in recognition prompting Mariah to put a finger up to her lips in a silence sign. He took the hint immediately with a nod of his head.

"What can I do for you, Miss?"

"Do you have a two-bedroom suite available? I'd like it for two nights and three days."

"So sorry but we only have a couple of those, and they are taken." His look told her how it concerned him to deliver this information.

"What I can do is give you two rooms on the top floor with an interior door to join both as one. Both rooms have views of the city, and beyond, these were reserved but canceled only a few moments ago. Would you like to see them?"

Mariah considered this quickly. She didn't want to be conspicuous or recognized by anyone else.

"I'll take them now and trust your judgment as to suitability. Please do not inform anyone that I am here otherwise we will have to leave."

"There is no way Miss; confidentiality is a must in my employment." He watched as she wrote her mothers maiden name to the guest registration book page.

Instructions were given for a Bellboy to follow Mariah and assist with baggage. Sarah had the most. Mariah and Fay still carried only a case each.

Tommy was fascinated with all, especially the strange gates on the hotel elevator. Mariah kept hold of his hand bending down occasionally to whisper something funny in his ear. His eyes shone with excitement as they came to a stop on their floor. Tommy pulled free of her hand, running ahead although not sure which direction to go.

Mariah held the room keys and opened the first one. The interconnecting door would need opening on both sides, so she proceeded to open the first before going to the second room. With doors accessible, there was plenty of space, and the view from the picture windows was spectacular.

Tommy stood staring down at the street far below. In his young life, he had never witnessed the likes. Wagons of goods, carriages, men on horseback, people walking and street sellers.

"So what do you think young man," Fay kneeled to his level placing an arm around him.

"I don't know if I am dreaming, cause it seems like it. But I don't want to wake up cause I like this castle and I know its magic."

Hearing his words struck Mariah, what she took for granted was unreal to the child. She hoped in time with his life improving that he always upheld the same enjoyment.

"Sarah, would you mind if I took Tommy to the shops with me? I'll need him for his clothing size."

"Oh but I can do that Mariah, there's no need for you too."

"I need to purchase other things for Fay and myself as well. Then later you two ladies can wander out and about. We don't need to draw attention to ourselves."

Fay looked at Sarah. "She's right you know, Sarah, we can both soak in the bath and let Mariah and Tommy have their turn later."

"Oh, such luxury and a bathroom each to spoil ourself.

That's fine Mariah take your time. You and Tommy can enjoy the same as us on your return." Sarah carried her daughter to the large bed and began removing her clothes as Mariah and Tommy walked out of the door.

 Holding the little boys' hand and talking to him as they went, Mariah walked slower to match his pace, while looking at a map of the town.

Her first stop was to be the shipping office to book seats down the river to Greensboro.

A paddle steamer sat at the side of the timbered dock, filling with merchandise and cargo or all shapes and sizes.

"Would you like to have a ride on a big boat like that one Tommy?" Mariah knew the answer but enjoyed his exhilaration.

"Oh yes, can we?"

"We will buy our tickets now, but you must not tell anyone except Mommy and Aunty Fay."

"Is Fay my aunty? I didn't have an aunt before. Can you be my aunty as well?"

"Of course I can dear, I would love to be, and I am so proud of the wonderful young man you are."

"Yes, I am a man," Tommy's chest puffed out with pride. "So I can keep secrets."

Mariah nodded with a smile and walking into the office to buy the tickets.

Chapter Five

Tommy Keeping Secrets

Walking back Tommy pointed to a shop selling small cups of ice-cream, or rather the children coming out from the building holding a paper cup and dipping a shaped wooden scoop into the thick consistency then popping it into their mouth.

"What are they eating Mariah," Tommy looked puzzled.

"Come, let's get you one, big man and then you can tell me if you like it."

Mariah was excited to see Tommy's face when experiencing his first taste. Holding his hand and swinging his arm they entered the store where a plump lady in a colorful dress served a little girl. This child fidgeted and whined, changing her mind continually about the flavor.

Leaving her parents to sort out what she wanted, the

shopkeeper turned with a smile to look at Tommy. "Show me which one you would like to try?"

Tommy looked at Mariah. "We will take two vanilla bean," Mariah made their choice.

"Does white taste nice Mariah? It looks like snow."

"You try it and tell me, Tommy."

Warily Tommy got some on his little scoop and tried. His face lit up with delight as he scooped more into his mouth to hold and enjoy the melting feel before swallowing.

"This is the nicest thing I have ever eaten." Mariah was informed.

His mouth was red from the cold when he reluctantly finished. Before it could be wiped clean, his shirt sleeve was raised to do the job. Mariah made a point to remember to buy Tommy handkerchiefs and explain how to use them.

Their next stop was a department store. They went

straight to the children's clothing purchasing a couple of dungarees and boys shirts for Rebbecca. Then it was Tommy's turn. The shop assistant looked down at him with distaste due to his soiled clothing.

Mariah took this in, staring in return at the girl without a word until she looked up and saw her customers disapproving face.

"Have you finished your scrutiny? If so I would like you to show me the latest clothes for this wonderful young man."

The girl's face reddened, "Certainly madam, come this way."

Mariah purchased three outfits with socks, shoes, and boots as well as a hat. Letting Tommy remain in one of the outfits she requested his old clothes to be packaged with the new and sent on to their hotel room, including those for his sister.

Tiredness settled in as the two shoppers returned to their hotel rooms. Excitedly, Tommy related their expedition to his mother while she bathed him. Eating his first ice-cream topped his list along with explaining how delicious the taste.

Mariah took her bath and then lay on the bed and slept. She didn't rouse with the knock on the door and delivery of the parcels. Knowing what they were, Fay took them to Sarah.

It was one in the afternoon before Fay woke her friend so that they could all go to lunch downstairs in the restaurant. Both children looked very different in their smart clothes, and their mother needed to update her's.

Rebbecca was a quiet little soul watching and listening while her big brother never seemed to stop talking. His enormous blue eyes looked around the dining room from the chandeliers that sparked with sunlight to the many diners and what they were eating.

*****

Giving Sarah money later to buy what else she needed, and a cap, shoes, and boots for Rebbecca. Mariah offered to mind the little girl while the women went out knowing it would help Sarah be free to try-on dresses.

Sarah looked relieved not to carry her daughter, and Tommy skipped happily along between both women to see the fantastic shops once more. He looked back once to see what Mariah was doing before she entered the hotel elevator.

Rebbecca was the sweetest toddler. She sat on the bedroom floor, taken with looking at herself in Mariah's hand mirror. Smiling at her reflection, she opened her mouth and stuck her tiny finger in to feel each tooth. Mariah guessed she had never seen herself until now.

Sitting down and reading the paper Mariah became engrossed, and Rebbecca was forgotten. Looking over at the little one, she no longer played. The mirror lay abandoned and sleep claimed the child right there on the floor.

"Oh goodness, you poor baby." Careful not to awaken her she was picked up and placed on the double bed. With pillows logged on either side, hopefully, there would be no falling off.

It was almost supper time when the three returned, all carrying parcels. Tommy looked tired but happy and wanted to show what his package contained for his sister.

"Mommy bought Rebbecca some more boys things; she told me it was a secret and not to tell anyone that she is a girl."

Mariah mouthed an OH, "Then why are you telling me Tommy?" she gave him her best-shocked look.

Tommy looked horrified. "I promise not to tell anyone else. You must keep this secret also Mariah," he added thoughtfully.

"HM, a good idea," she confirmed with a smile and ruffle of his hair.

Tommy skipped into the other bedroom to tell his mother that Mariah would also keep the secret. "But Mommy, Rebbecca is a girls name and people might laugh."

Sarah put her hand to her mouth, thinking, "such a bright boy. Now, let me see. A name beginning with R. What about Rebel?" She pretended the name just came to her.

"Rebel is a good name, I like it, but will Rebbecca always be called that?"

"No son, only for a little while, but we will be sure not to tell a living soul won't we?"

Nodding his head, Tommy assured he was a man who kept his word. All the women smiled at each other, what a treasure this seven-year-old was.

No more parcels opened, it was time to wash up, tidy hair and go downstairs for supper. Little Rebbecca was cutely dressed as a boy again with her curls tucked into the cap she wore.

"This is my brother Rebel," Tommy solemnly told their waiter. The waiter smiled in acknowledgment.

"I did it, "the little boy leaned over to whisper to his mother.

"Well done, but no more whispering now, its bad manners." Changing the subject at the sight of his crestfallen face, she added softly, "how would you like to eat beef stew? That sounds delicious doesn't it?"

The reprimand was forgotten, and he smiled, "yes I would like that."

With their meals delivered, all were quiet while enjoying the food.

 A small bowl of mash with beef stew arrived for Rebecca which her mother fed her in between eating her own.

Tommy sat proudly using his best manners, glancing around at the other patrons occasionally to see if anyone watched him. He and his sister were the only children present.

*****

The steamboat proved to be the most exciting trip of young Tommy's life. Three pairs of grown-up eyes kept watching him not to fall into the water as he leaned precariously over the side. An elderly gentleman found him to be a treat and enjoyed pointing out the different fish and telling Tommy their species. He was a pleasant man who introduced himself as Colonel Carson-Rigby late of the 7th North Carolina infantry regiment. "But we were later transferred to the army of North Virginia, becoming part of A. P. Hill's Light Division."

He nodded in memory. "AH yes, those days are long gone, but they always remain with you, keeping you humble." Mariah, Fay, and Sarah looked at him as he lowered his head in grieving memory. From all they had heard about the civil war, it was not an easy thing to forget.

"Where are your family Colonel Rigby?" Mariah asked

respectfully.

"Most are long gone," he looked at her offering no more and then looked back to where Tommy still watched the fish.

Feeling he was an honorable man and dependable, Mariah shared their destination. "I'm sure that since you're a traveler that you must know the place of my birth, Swansboro."

"Certainly my dear, I do. I live there to remain close to my only son; he's a lawyer in that town."

"Well, it looks as if we might be neighbors then."

"If you don't mind my saying young lady, you look familiar."

"Really," Miranda answered. "I have many people tell me that, I must have a typical face."

"Oh no my dear, you have the loveliest face, not typical at all."

A bell sounded for lunch, and Colonel Rigby looked up at the sound.

"Please come and sit with us for lunch Colonel," Miranda stood up and reached over to Tommy for his hand. "It's time to eat now big man."

"Are we eating fish? I saw a man with a line catching them?" He pointed to the rear end of the boat from where they stood.

The colonel laughed and ruffled Tommy's hair, "we best get to our table then and order, or they will be all eaten. Many folk love fresh fish."

No further persuasion was needed for them to leave their seats and walk to the dining room.

Chapter Six

A Shocking Difference

Greensboro, North Carolina was a thriving place having grown beyond Miranda's expectation in the last ten years.

They booked in at The Biltmore Hotel the only place to stay in the town. At a few years old everything was tasteful and immaculate.

The ladies discover that Greensboro was the hub for the Southern textile industry with large factories employing hundreds of workers. Since their steamboat didn't leave for Swansboro until noon the next day, it was decided to buy flannel and denim material to take with them. It would be cheaper than from a storekeeper and would come to good use. Miranda requested the large parcel to be delivered straight to their steamboat.

Colonel Rigby remained with them for the rest of the journey by water, as it was to take seven hours. He spent time talking and teaching Tommy about nature along the way. They enjoyed hearing his stories at the dining room table as they ate.

As Swansboro came into view that evening, the Colonel asked to speak with Mariah privately. Walking to stand by the disembarking rail Mariah was asked where her family plantation was situated. Wondering why he would ask Mariah felt reluctant to say. Peace descended over her with a knowing in her spirit that he was a friend and meant her no harm.

Still, she asked the question. "Why do you want to know?"

The colonel took her one hand in both of his as he looked the young woman in the eye. "Take care, my dear. Many unusual things have been happening in our town, strange occurrences. I don't wish to frighten you but please don't make any impulsive decisions that could prove a danger to you and your family. If you need help, don't fail to call on me. My son has his office in town, and occasionally I preside at the town court. It won't be hard to find me."

With a final shake of her hand in his, he carefully let it go. "Let's join the others. Do you have someone coming to pick you up?"

"I sent a telegram to my aunt, but if there is no one to meet us, we will have to hire a cab I guess."

"Hm, that could be difficult at this time of day. I have my man coming to collect me, so if no-one is there for you, we'll see you home."

As the steamer pulled in at the landing dock, it hit hard with a loud thump and a shake. Colonel reached out just in time to grab Tommy by the leg as he was flung wildly in the air. It was a subdued little boy close to tears from fright who shook from shock as the colonel hugged him tight before settling him back on the deck.

The colonel was a big man in height and size with large hands. With gray wavy hair worn to his collar, kind brown eyes and a ruddy complexion, his whole demeanor stood for security. Mariah's heart was still in her mouth with the knowledge that Tommy might have perished. Sarah's face resembled white stone, and she made no move to comfort her son, she was unable to due to the shock. Fay had been looking the other way, unaware of the near catastrophe.

Tommy looked at his mother still transfixed; he stared from her to Colonel Rigby. The little boy's eyes moved on to Mariah and Fay. Mariah was unsure how to act, then felt in her heart to leave Tommy where he was, with his protector.

Looking to the colonel who looked back at him Tommy remembered what he should do as a gentleman. He held out his little hand to be clasped and shook by his rescuer.

"Thank you, Sir," Tommy whispered weakly. "I guess it was silly to lean over the boat like that. But I'll never do it again, I promise."

"I know you won't Tommy," his protector smiled, placing his hand momentarily on the boys head.

People spilled down the gangplank pushing and shoving to be first off. Carrying something each of Sarah's and their bag, Mariah and Fay held back. Sarah held Rebel and her carpet bag while Tommy and the colonel both had hold of Sarah's more substantial case. The Colonel bore the weight, carrying his small port in his other hand.

Disembarked and walking upstairs from the dock to the road a carriage and a wagon sat waiting. Hopping down from the cart and stirring up the dirt, was a dark-skinned young man. He scanned the faces of women passing, unsure of who he was to collect.

Mariah wasn't shy to approach and inquire if he came from Fairways Plantation.

"Sure thing, I'm from there and sent here to collect the niece of Miss. Milly. Are you her?"

"Yes I am," Mariah replied thankfully turning back to the women. "Can you put all of our things in the back of the cart please er, what is your name?"

"It's Noah Randal. My wife, Tilly is Miss. Milly's cook."

"Well Noah, my name is Mariah, and these are my friends, Miss. Fay Gates and Mrs. Sarah Yarman. Oh, and this young man is Tommy. I believe he would like to sit up front with us."

Tommy looked up at Noah and then offered his hand to shake before he was lifted high up onto the front wagon seat.

With goodbyes and thank you to their new male friend Sarah and Fay climbed up to sit on the back seat with little Rebel who was handed up once they settled.

Mariah climbed up to sit beside Tommy.

It took almost an hour to reach Fairways and beginning to get dark as they turned in at the front gate. Built on the crest of a hill stood the magnificent two-story structure, appearing ghostly in the dimming light.

The dilapidated sight that met her eyes shocked Mariah

to the core.

Peeling house paint and a part of the roof hanging broken at one side of the porch made all look sad from the lack of care. The once pristine grounds lay in disorder with overgrown weeds. The flower beds were gone and forgotten.

"What's happened here Noah this is unacceptable."

"What you mean Miss.?" Noah frowned as if Mariah asked a strange question.

"What do I mean? Why Fairways is unkempt and running to ruin this isn't how it was, what has happened here? And what exactly is your job, Noah?"

"Well, I feed the animals, milk the cow tend the vegetable garden and such like."

The wagon pulled up near the front stairs. Miranda got down and lifted Tommy to set him on the ground. She felt angry and showed it. "Help the ladies and bring in our belongs." She ordered Noah.

Someone was accountable for this mess and Mariah tended to find out who. She suspected Noah for one wasn't pulling his weight.

Running up the stairs and over the porch to the front door, the latch was locked. Mariah thumped on the paneling and called out to her aunt.

"Who you be?" An unfamiliar voice yelled from inside.

"I am Mariah Kingsford who belongs here, where is my Aunt Milly, open up this door at once."

Noise and the juggling of keys followed before the door opening a crack. A dark face peered out, and Mariah guessed this to be Noah's wife.

"Are you Tilly?"

"Yes, Mam."

"Well open the door! It's been a long trip, and we're all tired. I certainly hope you have supper prepared?"

Mariah pushed the door inwards sighting an untidy

mess everywhere.

"Where is my aunt?" she demanded. Walking and looking around at what had once been immaculate, she was astounded by the dirty chaos.

Without waiting on an answer, and picking up her skirts, she ran up the stairs to where she remembered her aunt slept.

It was bewildering, with no lamps lit or friendly welcome home, nothing but silence. Mariah burst into her aunt's old room and found her laying on a dirty bed looking unkempt and in disarray. Shaking her aunt's shoulder, Mariah called her name with little response.

"Aunty, Aunty, it's me, Mariah, what are you doing here like this, are you ill? what has happened here.?"

Gradually her aunt seemed to come out of her fog, opening her eyes and looking at Mariah as one in a stupor. She kept on staring until a light turned on within. Her hand reached to touch Mariah's face, and she blinked while trying to focus. "Mariah, is that you

Mariah?"

"Yes Aunty it's me, Mariah and I am home to stay. Come, dear, get up and come downstairs it looks like this place needs a good shake-up, and I'll be the one to get it on the move."

Mariah turned on the bedroom gas light doing the same in the hall. "Enough of this darkness! Come Aunt we have visitors and need to welcome and feed them." She ushered her aunt beside her holding her by the arm while maneuvering down the stairs.

Chapter Seven

Dealing with Dishonesty

Everyone was standing in the downstairs entry hall including Noah and Tilly. Mariah was furious, so angry one fist clenched tightly by her side. Remembering the Colonel's words not to act impulsively, she prayed in her mind for wisdom. She would wait for the morning before grilling the staff. Tonight she needed to be civil.

"Right, first of all. Tilly, have you got a meal ready for us?"

"Well sort of Mam, there be cornbread, and we got ham and fried potato."

"Right" ordered Miranda, "get it served in the dining room and make sure the table is clean before it's laid out. You can help her Noah."

She thought she was going to get a back-answer from Noah. His mouth opened, and a scowl flooded his face. Seeing a warning look from his wife: he changed his mind.

Turning to Fay and Sarah, Mariah shook her head in exasperation before remembering to introduce her aunt.

Fay put her case down walking to Mariah and putting her arm around her; she understood her friend's shock. "We'll get it all cleaned up don't worry Mariah, soap, and water do wonders."

Then Fay politely kissed Milly's cheek, "It's a pleasure to meet you, Miss. Milly."

"Let's get our bags upstairs and find our bedrooms," Mariah took control. "I'll take my grandparent's old room right at the end of the hall."

Seating her aunt on a chair in the dining room, Mariah gently told her to wait as she'd be back soon. Then the others were led upstairs.

Opening bedroom doors Mariah felt thankful to find that everything in the unused rooms had protected covering. Whipping off dust sheets from furniture and beds she appreciated nothing looked as bad as downstairs. On pulling back the layers and quilt of the first bed, it was clean yet smelled musty. Windows were thrown open to refreshen the rooms, and bags left behind in their allocations. Closing the doors again they trooped in line downstairs.

Aunt Milly sat at the dining room table watching it set with the scarce meal. There was milk to drink so that would help satisfy. They took their time, and before finished, Tommy was yawning with Rebel asleep on her mother lap.

"You go on up to bed, Sarah, and look after yourself and the children. Tomorrow we'll take a better look around." Sarah gave no resistance and took off with Tommy hanging onto her skirt to help pull him up the stairs.

Mariah looked at Fay. "There's one thing I want to do tonight, and that's giving my aunt a bath."

Fay nodded in agreement looking into her eyes. "What

would you like me to do dear?"

"I would love you to make her bed with fresh sheets please Fay; you'll find linen in that large cupboard in the first room at the right of the stairs."

"Sure, that's fine I'll find them."

Rising from the table, Fay headed off. Mariah took her aunts' hand and beckoning with her other. "Come, Aunt Milly, it's time for a nice bath."

Walking through the kitchen Noah and Tilly sat at a table eating fried chicken. *What was going on here?* Both had the grace to look guilty. They hadn't expected Mariah catch them.

Standing and looking at the food Mariah questioned, " where did you get that chicken?"

Noah answered boldly, "I killed it today."

"So why did we not have that for our dinner tonight?"

Neither answered.

"I'll see you two in the morning. I want a decent breakfast on the table at eight sharp." She trotted off to the bathroom lighting the gas heater first to warm the water. There was no need for it to be hot as the night was mild.

Mariah couldn't work out what the matter was with her aunt? She seemed to have no will and reminded Mariah of a old person with mind absence. She decided to test her cognitive understanding by giving a command.

"Okay Aunty, take those clothes off, and we'll get you into the bath." Mariah turned her back to bend over the tub and fit the plug. Warm water flowed as soon as the tap turned.

She hoped to see her aunt ready when turning back. "How are you going Aunt Milly? Oh, do you need help dear?"

Her aunt stood watching as if unsure of what to do. Gently Mariah removed her clothing then helped her into the water. At half full, the water was turned off. It was a hip-bath so safe to leave Milly soaking while going to find a clean nightgown. Running upstairs and into her aunt's room, she was quick to rummaging and discover what she wanted.

Fay busily stripped the bed and applied fresh sheets with an open window.

 Alone to talk for the first time since arriving the two women looked at each other. "You didn't expect this did you, Mariah?"

"No Fay, I was stunned, but I'll look well into this problem in the morning. That bed smells fresher. If you feel like a bath, we will finish shortly. The bathing room is just off the kitchen."

"Tonight I'll do with a wash," Fay shook her head. "Tomorrow will be time enough."

"Okay, well I'm off to get my aunt out, dressed and to bed. I'll see you in the morning."

*****

At eight sharp the next morning, Mariah walked into the kitchen to find Tilly preparing to carry the last of the cooked breakfast to the dining room. The family sat waiting, but Noah was nowhere in sight.

"Good Tilly, I see you are trying. Where is Noah?"

Tilly looked frightened and stared without answering.

"I asked you a question Tilly, where is your husband?"

"I don't know Mam; he milked the cow collected the eggs and then took off as usual."

Mariah's annoyance reflected on her face. "So he is in the habit of not being here to tend his work is that what you are telling me?"

"I suppose so Mam, but please don't tell him I told you as he will get furious."

Mariah thought about this. It seemed Noah was a

problem and needed reprimanding. She would play it wise and go to see Colonel Rigby about him tomorrow. Noah would not be getting away with bullying in this house any longer.

With a deep breath, Mariah smiled a Good Morning to everyone, glad to see her aunt looking more awake, clean and tidy. Mariah took the chair at the head of the table.

Fay looked at her and then her aunt giving the nod. Mariah knew it was she who had roused and dressed her relative.

Tommy, as usual, talked nonstop before his mother told him that a gentleman did not speak while eating. Tommy sat up tall in his chair to show he understood.

"How are you this morning, Aunt Milly?" Reaching across Mariah covered her aunt's hand with her own.

"Well my head is a little clearer, Noah didn't give me my medicine last night, I don't know why." Mariah and Fay looked at each other.

"What medicine is that Aunt?"

"Why it's to make me sleep so that I don't have nightmares."

"You have been having nightmares? What have they been about?"

"Nothing for you to worry over Mariah, I didn't have it last night and perhaps now with you and these lovely friends here, it will probably stop."

Mariah looked around the table at the other two women. Sarah caught her eye and then quickly looked toward the dining room open door. A glimpse of someone hurriedly retreating captured Mariah's interest.

So they were being watched were they?

She gave Sarah a conspiring nod and smile. Then diplomatically changed the subject.

"We are going to have a busy day today, so wear old clothes. We'll each change our beds with clean linen then, Fay, Tilly, and I can commence putting things right down here."

Sarah looked bewildered at not being included. "I must do my share, Mariah."

"Yes, Sarah, I haven't forgotten you. Your job will be the nursery, cleaning it and changing the cot and bed linens, you may have noticed an extra door in your room. In case you didn't look…..," Sarah shook her head no. "Then you will find it goes straight into the children's room where there are lots of things to keep Tommy and *Rebel* happy."

Tommy looked up, eyes shining. "What kind of things Aunt Mariah?"

It was a delight to hear him call her aunt, Mariah smiled at him. "Why Mr. Tommy, everything is a secret for you to discover and take good care of with your little *brother*."

She winked at him in secret put her finger over her lips while casting a glance toward the doorway. The little boy winked back with both eyes, then sat trying to learn how to do it with only one eyelid.

"What am I to do Mariah? You are the head of the house now, and I am happy for you to take over. Fathers lawyer Mr. Carson-Rigby wants to see you by the way."

"Oh really? Well, I will do that tomorrow as well. I can take you with me. I'm sure you will enjoy an outing."

"Oh yes Mariah," she clapped her hands, "I can't remember when I last went to town."

With breakfast over, each one, including her aunt took off to fulfill their assignments. Fay was to keep an eye on Milly while tending to her room.

By evening the inside of the house should be put to rights again Mariah surmised. Now it was time to have a word with Tilly and Noah.

Entering the kitchen, Tilly sat alone finishing off her breakfast. "We need to talk Tilly."

The other woman looked frightened and glanced around

probably hoping for Noah to appear. She kept shuffling her feet with nerves.

Mariah was not going to be lenient. "I am utterly shocked at the condition of this house, Tilly.

How much is your monthly pay?" When Tilly mentioned an amount, it was more than suitable for the house to be kept in better condition.

"So why is it that you haven't been adequately up keeping what you are paid to do?"

Tilly's eye's looked down, and she silently shook her head unable to find an excuse.

Chapter Eight

A Very Evil Man

Tilly's face displayed shame, and finally, as Mariah waited, she explained. "No-one ever comes here, and Noah says we shouldn't have to work our fingers to the bone for no good reason."

"Oh he does, does he. Well firstly Noah is not the master here, and secondly, you do the work you are paid to do. Taking advantage of people is dishonest and people who are dishonest get in trouble with the law, do you understand me, Tilly?"

"Yes, Mam. I don't want no trouble with the law."

"Where is Noah and when will he be home?"

Tilly shook her head. "He goes off for days sometimes and leaves me to take care of things. I am the one to give Miss. Milly her medicine when he's not here."

Mariah tapped her fingers on the table-top with

annoyance. "I'd like to see that medicine, Tilly."

Rising from her seat, Tilly walked to a cupboard, opened it and withdrew a bottle. She stepped back, handing it over to Mariah before sitting again.

Mariah stared at the label.

It read **Laudanum.**

Noah Randal

Take with care as needed.

Mariah shook her head in disbelief. That evil man was sedating her aunt. The medicine prescribed, was for him, but he likely got it to keep Aunt Milly in a state of slumber. What was his reason for this? How dare he.

"What does the label on this bottle say?" She turned it for Tilly to see. After looking for a moment, Tilly responded. "I can't read Miss. likely it says, Miss. Milly's name?"

"Well," Mariah got up, "when Noah comes in I'd like you

to tell him I want to see him. Don't mention that I have this bottle as we don't want him to be angry with YOU do we?"

Tilly's looked petrified, "No Mam! I don't want to get him riled."

Mariah walked off with the bottle; she knew where to hide it. Somewhere it wouldn't be found. From her evaluation of the events in this house, Noah was an evil man.

Noah did not return that day nor in the evening for which Mariah was thankful as she didn't want to be the one to deal with him. There was a strange mystery about that man, and it caused her skin to creep.

Immediately following breaking fast the next morning, Mariah went to the barn to hitch the horse and buggy. With the amount of food and water laid out for the animal, it was apparent Noah intended to be gone for another day at least.

Fay helped Milly to dress in a blue tailored morning outfit, styling her fair hair and pinning on a wide-brimmed straw hat with a blue feather, it was complimented to perfection.

Milly's blue eyes twinkled while viewing her reflection in a full-length mirror. Turning this way and that, she observed every angle. "My, I haven't looked this grand in a long time. My sister, Mariah's mother, sent me this, isn't it pretty?"

Fay agreed that it was and looking at Milly's slim body and pretty face Fay left it sad for her denied marriage in her youth.

Mariah had to put the black dress on again as it was the best she had until their chest arrived. But she dressed it up with a pink hat and big ornamental pink topaz pin displayed on the front bodice. Both ladies looked arresting as they departed for a morning in town.

Milly spoke about many things on the way. "I've had no will to do anything for a few months now Mariah. I am so glad that you are here and will finally take hold of your inheritance."

"What inheritance is that Aunt Milly?" Mariah pulled back on the horse's reins as they approached the town.

"Why your grandfather left you everything didn't your parents tell you? The house, and land. I was given an allowance just as your mother was, but you hold control of the property, Mariah."

This was news and something Mariah knew the lawyer would help her to understand. She'd wait until hearing it off him as her aunt might still be confused. Why hadn't her parents spoken of it if so? Probably not to deter her career.

"What is this lawyer like in age? Young or old?

"Well, he is younger than Mr. Barret who was there before him, and who occasionally stands in when Mr. Carson–Rigby needs to travel for business.

"Rigby? I met a Colonel Rigby on the way here. I

remember him saying something about his son. He said I could make contact through him if I needed."

"Oh yes, I believe the colonel is a nice man although it's been many years since I last saw him."

Mariah pulled the horse up right in front of the lawyer's office, situated beside a pharmacy. Tying the reins to the hitching rail both ladies trooped noisily up the wooden upstairs to his office.

A male secretary sat at a desk in the room they entered. He looked up over his spectacles as Mariah approached.

"Hello, I'd like to see the lawyer if possible."

"Yes, Mam, can I have your name?"

"I am the granddaughter of Charles Segal, and my name is Mariah Kingsford."

Her grandfather name brought a quizzing expression to the man's face. "Mr. Carson is currently busy, but he shouldn't take long. Would you ladies care to take a seat?"

They sat quietly together until the inner door opened and Colonel Rigby emerged with his son behind.

Surprise lit the Colonel's face and he walked straight towards her. "Well Mariah, I didn't expect to see you this soon."

"I am so glad that you are here Colonel, and this is my aunt, Miss. Milly Segal," she introduced them.

"It's a pleasure to make your acquaintance again dear lady; it has been a few years I believe."

"Yes it has, I didn't expect you would remember who I am," Milly blushed.

"How could I not remember a southern beauty such as yourself?" His eyes lit on Milly with interest. "You ladies must call me Jeb; we are friends now I hope."

As the women began to protest, he held up both hands to stop them. "No, no, I insist on my first name."

Turning to his son, he introduced them both. Mariah stared at his son's face remembering him as that handsome man from the train. He stared back holding her gaze with an amused smile. It caused a dimple to dance in one cheek.

"It's nice to meet you again Miss. Kingsford, are you here to see my father or me?" He raised an eyebrow looking straight at her while waiting for a reply.

Her face heated, and she took a moment to answer. "Both Mr. Carson-Rigby, you were my grandfather's lawyer I believe."

"Ah yes," He guided her into his office then turned to his father. "Don't go too far Pa; it looks like you are needed as well."

"I'll sit here with Miss. Milly and keep her company while Dennis gets us both a cup of tea."

Seated across from the lawyer Mariah got straight to the

point. "I believe you to be the guardian of my grandfather's estate Mr. Carson–Rigby."

"I am that. I go only by Carson, Miss. Kingsford, except on legal forms, otherwise it's too much of a mouth full."

He sat back in his chair observing her thoroughly. "So you are back at your family home? That's good, and I hope you stay, the place needs a strong hand. Now, about the Will. Your grandfather left all of his possessions to you." He got up and walked to a file.

"I have kept you a copy as I'm sure you would like to appraise it. You'll find everything in order. There is also a monthly allowance for running the house and paying wages. You need never worry about how to manage."

Mariah placed the copy in her reticule to read later at home.

"Thank you, Mr. Carson. Now I'd like to know a little more about the two people working for my aunt, Tilly, and Noah Randal?"

"It's Tilly Jones and Noah Randal, Miss. Kingsford, they are not married."

"Oh,… I was led to believe they were married. Well, never mind that, the problem is both have been slovenly and not done the work they are paid to do."

Hart Carson sat forward in his chair on hearing this. "I employed both. Tilly has been working there for about five years and was always articulate in her cleaning and care. Noah was employed about four months ago after old Ben Dyer passed away. I haven't been out to see the place of late so know nothing about it not being satisfactory."

"Well, it's not. I couldn't believe the state of disarray I saw when arriving home. To add to that Noah has been drugging my aunt with laudanum, prescribed for him, and not her."

The lawyer was staring at her stunned. "I have never had a problem with anyone employed by me before this. Actually, it was my secretary Dennis who suggested

Noah. If Noah isn't what he should be, then I must wonder if Dennis is either." Hart looked shocked.

Mariah could have added she didn't like the look of his secretary but held her tongue. "That's not a nice thought, and you could very well be right."

"What do you want to do about Noah and Tilly?"

"I will keep Tilly as it seems Noah oppresses her. With him, I was hoping your father could come and get him to leave. I want him gone from my home."

"That sounds like it will work. I prefer my father take a couple of his farm hands with him in case of trouble. He may also know of someone honest to replace Noah."

"Thank you, Mr. Carson, I'll take your advice, and I'll ask your father to come downstairs so that I can talk to him without Dennis nearby."

Before seeing Mariah out, Hart informed her that he'd visit in a couple of days to make sure everything was sorted and running smoothly.

He wanted to see more of Miss. Mariah Kingsford, and the thought of being able to have a reason, now delighted him.

Chapter Nine

Midnight Noises

Colonel or Jeb as they were to call him now, announced he would be at Fairways the next morning bringing two men with him who had been requesting work. The only persons besides Mariah who knew he was coming and why, were Fay and Milly. They knew it was imperative not to say a thing as Mariah wasn't entirely sure about Tilly.

After collecting her chest from the train station, the women enjoyed a leisurely ride back home. Milly was not her usual talkative self this time. Instead, she sat in a dreamy state with a smile on her lips for most of the return trip.

With Noah gone it was Fay who assisted Mariah with bringing the trunk inside. They decided it was more convenient to take their clothes out downstairs then stow the chest in the sitting room.

Next, Tilly was requested to clean the two spare rooms in the servants' quarters. These were on the opposite side of the home to the kitchen and bathroom. Tilly didn't question why and Mariah gave no reason.

Sarah's two children found the nursery a delight to play and sleep in, which had them busy. Young Tommy kept making discoveries of toys in the toy chest and cupboard. He took to carrying a toy gun around everywhere with him. Rebel, held a ball in both hands keeping her enthralled when it dropped and bounced. With a squeal, she toddled after it grinning to show her pearly teeth.

Mariah worked out a schedule of duties for Sarah placing her as the housekeeper over Tilly. Sarah was to take Saturday afternoon and Sunday as her days off and Tilly just Sunday. Sarah was thrilled with the arrangement and with her wage. She would continue to have her meals with Mariah as part of the family.

The next day was Friday, and Noah arrived back at the plantation around ten o'clock walking into the kitchen with a smug look on his face. Jeb and the two men were in the dining room having a cup of tea and cake. On spying Noah, Mariah hurried to tell Jeb where he was, sitting in the kitchen waiting for Tilly to preparing him breakfast.

"This is what we'll do Mariah. You go in and confront him about his work ethic. These men and I will wait and listen just outside of the door. If he minds you and is prepared to accept what you say, I will walk in to talk to you as if I don't know what's going on. BUT, should he give any trouble, then the three of us will come and back you."

Mariah gave a weak smile and nodded in agreement. Hopefully, there would be no problems. She walked in hurriedly as if she had no idea Noah had returned. Seated at the table, she approached with a frown.

"What are you doing here Noah?"

"I work here," his sneer challenged her to try to

reprimand his attitude.

"Not anymore you don't," Mariah stood with her hands on her hips. "You were absent for three days, and I don't pay you to go off as the desire strikes you."

"You are not my boss. Miss. Milly is, and she will keep me."

"Miss. Milly does not own this house, I do, and your wage comes to you in goodwill for work done well. No work, no wage! You can pack up your things and go."

"I'm staying you silly woman, and if I ever do go, I will take my wife with me."

He looked over at Tilly cringing near the stove.

"You are mistaken Mr.! you are going now, and since my lawyer confirmed you two are not married, Tilly remains here. You have no command over her."

Noah arose, his face threatening, and a fist lifted shaking in the air. "You can't make me!" He yelled.

Jeb and his two men appeared. "Who do you think you are?" Jeb stormed. "When the person who pays your wage tells you to go, then you go. So are you going to leave peacefully or do I take you to the sheriff for abusing the ladies in their home, and, for giving, Miss. Milly an illegal drug?"

Noah's whole demure changed when seeing Jeb. "Why she bring you here Judge, I didn't do anything. The medicine given to Miss. Milly was to help her sleep, nothing else."

Jeb stared him in the eye. "Don't try to play me for a fool. It was prescribed medication for you, not for her. You are not a doctor and neither can you take it upon yourself to act like one. You have ten minutes to get your things together and leave. Otherwise, you are going to see yourself on the wrong side of the law." Jeb's voice was deadly; he meant business and Noah knew it.

Looking at Tilly, he ordered her to go and get his clothes.

Jeb roared at him like a wild bull, "get them yourself you lazy young whelp. Help him out of here boys."

Tilly looked terrified, so Mariah sent her to go and begin cleaning the dining room. She was better out of the way than to be tormented by evil looks from Noah on his return.

Appearing again carrying a bundle Noah swung quickly out of the back door with the two men close behind.

"Make sure you never approach this property again, or you'll face the consequences," Jeb yelled at Noah's back.

Mariah took a deep breath, she was shaken and hoped she'd seen the last of Noah Randal, yet she had a bad feeling he'd be back.

"Thank you so much," she looked at Jeb. "Can I do

anything for you."

He mused, thinking for a moment. Then decided to speak his mind.

"Well come to think of it young lady I believe you can. I'd like to keep dropping in to see Milly if you don't mind, I think we would enjoy one another's southern company."

A smile came to Mariah's face, "I can't think of anything I would like better. I'll call her down now, and we'll all have more tea."

Jeb stood in the foyer waiting and wasn't disappointed as Milly soon descended the stairs. "Mariah says we are going to have tea and that you would like to hear me play the piano after."

"That would be very nice of you Miss. Milly, the big man, stood back for the ladies to enter the dining room first, then he hurried to pull a chair out for each of them.

Supper was a happy affair that evening with Jeb driving back to his home soon after. "While it's still daylight and these old eyes can see," he chuckled.

"Are you sure you'll be safe, I don't like to think Noah might be lurking somewhere.

Jeb laughed. "I have a gun and know how to use it, my dear. I'll be home in half an hour. Miss. Milly has agreed to attend church with me on Sunday morning, so I'll be back then."

With a wave, he drove down the driveway.

Fay and Milly went upstairs to their rooms while Mariah walked to the kitchen.

Tilly sat quietly eating while the new workers talked. Mariah sat down with them and extended her arm around Tilly's shoulder.

"Tilly, don't be afraid and if Noah tries to contact you, you must tell me. We have these two big men here now to protect us."

She turned to the men. "Jeb told me you both need work, so I'm willing to take you on, there's a lot to be done around here. Two things though, no drinking or bad language. I am not a slave driver, but neither am I a pushover."

"No worries Mam, we are Christian men and don't do those things, anyway."

"Good, you have Saturday afternoon and Sunday free from work. Your wage is ten dollars a week each, payable monthly. You get free board and meals, plus a bonus if required for anything extra, how is that?"

"That's more than reasonable thank you. My name is Will, and this here is my cousin Brian. Our surname is Bonett. We will be happy to work here. For the last few years, we've worked in a Kentucky coal mine, and it almost killed Brian."

"So how old are you both?"

Will answered again. "I'm thirty-six, and Brian here is twenty- nine, we got orphaned when our family home burnt down years past. This here will be the best job and chance we have had so far; we won't let you down."

Mariah smiled, "I am certain that you won't. Tilly will show you to your rooms when you are ready. I'm off to bed so I'll see you all in the morning."

Walking into her bedroom, locking the door and drawing the drapes Mariah went straight to inspect her grandfather's secret hideout. He showed her this before she left home at sixteen. Swearing her to secrecy, he said she was the only person other than himself to know of it. In a corner... at the side of a vast wardrobe hidden in its shadow was the narrow, door. Wallpaper the same design as the rest of the room blended over it well. Opening it, Mariah peered within before stepping inside.

It smelled musty as expected, taking a lamp hanging on the wall she lit it proceeding six feet along the narrow passage before stairs descended far down beneath ground level. Along another passageway and she was able to look through a grate into the cellar. Included at the end of this passageway was a tiny cell type room containing a bed. Mariah shuddered aware this place had been for an unpleasant purpose.

 Due to darkness, nothing was seen in the cellar. Deciding to return in the daylight from the kitchen entrance, Mariah retraced her steps, not liking to wander around at night.

She also knew of a hidden tunnel that led from the cellar about a mile underground through the hill from the house. She knew that It opened into the back of a secret cave. It was another mystery to be solved, but for now, she'd return to her room.

After dimming the lamps, the drapes on all three walls were re-opened. Stifling a yawn, Mariah climbed into the four-poster bed to say her prayers and fall into immediate slumber.

Hours later she awoke with pounding on her bedroom door. Her aunt's voice called her name in panic. "Mariah open the door and let me in."

Half asleep Mariah opened the door to have Milly fall hysterically into her arms. Then Mariah heard the sounds. Horses, many horses, riding around the house. They stopped and then went around once more.

Running to the window and looking down the horsemen appeared like swirling black shadows. Unreal and ghostly, yet Mariah knew they were devil riders. Men out at night doing what they shouldn't, here at the family plantation where they had no right to trespass.

Her heart pounded. She wondered if Will and Brian had heard and stirred awake. If her aunt hadn't raised her, Mariah would likely still be cuddled up in sleep.

"It's okay Aunt Milly, here, come to my bed with me." Taking her aunts hand and leading her over Mariah sat her down, lifting her legs under the covers.

"We are fine dear one; all the doors are safely locked so no one can get inside. You're safe in here with me."

The horses could now be heard thundering away but who were they and what business did they have here? She would bring this new event to Jeb's attention, something was wrong, and Mariah had a feeling that whatever it was, Noah was involved.

Her aunt slept peacefully by her side and Mariah decided that until this mystery was solved and over, her aunt could continue to sleep with her.

The next morning no one mentioned having heard horse riders. Mariah said nothing keeping silent, preferring not to cause alarm. She would wait until she spoke to Jeb tomorrow before she addressed the new workmen. Meanwhile, she'd keep it to herself.

Chapter Ten

Keeping Secure

It was ten years since Mariah had been taught to use a gun; she knew where they were stored and would retrieve a couple to use if those riders appeared again. Yes, she would be ready with grandfathers, Henry repeating rifle. Not to harm but to frighten them.

She needed to practice, but where? The old quarry where her grandfather taught her was safe, and she wasn't likely to accidentally shoot anyone.

Being encouraged to pray about this first Mariah returned to her room locking the door and kneeling beside her bed.

Dear Lord, am I thinking clearly? I am unsure what to do, yet I want to keep my little family safe. I understand now how terrified my aunt was as my own heart

thumped with fear at the sight of those riders. I need to
get closer to you Lord, and I ask that you show me what I
am to do, In Jesus' name. Amen.

Mariah kept on kneeling and gradually as she waited, peace washed over her. She felt a knowing in her soul that God had heard her, so she remained where she was in obedience, waiting on a reply.

Her eyes whipped open with the sensation of not being alone. The most incredible being ever, stood in the room, shining with an ethereal glow. Mariah thought her heart would stop; such was her wonder. Then a voice entered her mind. "The Lord is with thee Mariah, trust in him with all thine heart. Don't lean on thine own understanding."

She was confused, perplexed, yes, she wanted to trust yet with what she'd witness with those horsemen how could she? These thoughts flooded her mind.

"Go to the cellar, your answer as to why the horsemen come is there. They create noise and fear as a distraction. Do nothing. No guns and no action, you will know what you are to do. Then you are to obey."

The image faded away yet peace remained.

"Thank you, Lord, Thank you," came Mariah's honest reply.

"You are to listen to the spirit and not act in the flesh." He spoke a final word.

With a stirring in her blood, Mariah quickly reacted. Up off the floor she dressed in her fathers pants and shirt then placing her feet into the old pair of boots she fled downstairs, the cellar her destination.

Tilly was nervous and perhaps rightly so, she fluttered after Mariah trying to persuade her not to go down into its depths.

"There are evil things down there Miss. Mariah, they will take your spirit and make you a zombie."

Mariah stopped to look at her. "What makes you think that Tilly? Has it happened to anyone before?"

"Not that I know of Miss., but Noah scared me bad about it, and I never go anywhere near there." Tilly was visibly shaking with fear.

"Honestly Tilly, don't believe everything you hear. Didn't you go down there before Noah came here?

"No Miss., cause the older cook who was here at that time would go. I was never allowed."

Mariah looked at her, then proceeded to open the cellar door. "This door is supposed to be locked, I'll slam the bolt when I come back up, and then it stays locked when I'm not here."

"Yes Mam, it will."

With a lamp lit at the entrance giving off enough light to get downstairs another light soon illuminated the floor. Mariah looked around with her mouth open. Stacks of wooden boxes lined the floor reaching almost to the ceiling, with bottles of liquid packed in tightly. Since there was no way Mariah could lift a box down to look inside, she went to call Will and Brian.

*****

"I think I know what that liquid is without even looking," Will voiced his opinion. His cousin Brian nodded in agreement.

Mariah felt the same, yet she had to check and make sure.

With a box down Brian opened a jar to smell inside before passing it to Mariah and Will.

"Yep, can't mistake that. Someone is using your cellar for illegal purposes Miss. Mariah.

A message came flowing into her mind. *'Check the inside bolt on the outside door.'*

She went straight there to look, and both bolts, top, and bottom were undone. So this was how they gained entry. She was very sure if she went outside and down the stairs to the cellar entrance, the door would be bolted. Immediately she shot both bolts home.

Mariah shivered. She knew whoever gained entrance

from outside, into the cellar could also go upstairs and gain entry to the rest of the house via the kitchen.

Giving a big sigh, she now knew they weren't safe. In future, all locks would be checked every night for security. She would put the new men in charge of making sure of that.

"What do you want to do about this lot Miss. Mariah?" Brian stood watching and waiting while Will counted the boxes to work out how many jars they contained. "I'd say there would be at least four thousand jars here, Miss." Will now stood back beside Brian to hear their instructions.

Mariah was thinking; she prayed in her mind. The answer came, *'let the law handle this it's not your problem, it's far too big for you to handle.'*

After telling the men she wanted them to check the bolts in the cellar, and the rest of the house every night, and not to mention the find to anyone. She concluded that the sheriff would know best what to do.

"Will, I want you to ride for him now, tell him I said, there is something here that needs his immediate attention. Brian, I want you to ride and tell Colonel Jeb the same. I will show and tell them when they arrive. I don't want anyone to overhear about this; it's too risky so be careful."

Three seriously thinking people ascended the stairs together. Mariah shot that bolt home as soon as they were through, securing the lock as they watched.

Both men took off on their errands while their mistress informed Tilly she was not to undo the cellar bolt for any reason. Tilly shook her head looking scared while asking. "Did you see a zombie, Miss. Mariah?"

"I'll not answer that just now Tilly, but there is something evil down there, and you need to keep the door fastened."   Since it was late afternoon, she added, "cook extra for tonight as we will have two or more extra for supper." The look on her mistresses face sent Tilly scurrying.

*****

Jeb arrived first with one of his work hands, reassuring Mariah that the man was trustworthy. The sheriff and his deputy came shortly after. All together they descended the cellar stairs.

On sighting the boxes and contents, Jeb spoke, "well Sheriff Taylor it seems we have discovered the secret mystery in this town. Lots of people are involved with such a considerable haul."

"I believe you're correct Jeb, and it's been going on for at least a year. I believe they likely smuggled it out by boat along the coastline. On Monday I'll do some checking to see what vessels pass through here, and when."

"Excellent." Jeb agreed.

"We need to leave the Moonshine here for the moment Miss. Mariah, sorry about that but this needs us to make a careful plan. Total secrecy is to be upheld so no talking to anyone, any of you. The walls have ears."

The sheriff concluded with, "we will only discuss what's to be done somewhere in the open, so nothing gets overheard."

Jeb turned to Mariah, "you are going to have to be a brave lady, and I believe you are. I will loan you two more of my men to stay in the barn every night until this is over. They will be of no inconvenience for you, arriving and departing in the cover of darkness. You won't even be aware of them. All the culprits need to be apprehended, and that can only happen with informed planning."

Mariah felt terrified until she remembered the angel. God would look after them, and as long as the sheriff and Jeb knew about this, there was no more for her to do, except for one thing while they were still in the cellar.

"I'd like that heavy barrel pushed against the outer door

to give extra strength while you men are here to handle it. But leave the door bolts visible, so we know they are secure."

"Bright idea," Jeb nodded, "right boys, let's see to it."

With all the muscle power the barrel was carefully walked-rolled until in place. Mariah sighed with relief. No-one could move that door now. All walked silently upstairs and once in the kitchen again; the men were invited to remain for supper.

Retiring to bed that night Mariah advised all to lock their bedroom doors as a safety precaution. "We are only women and children sleeping up here, and it won't hurt to be careful."

Chapter Eleven

Vigilant Safeguarding

The next day being Sunday, Tilly and the cousins had the day off. Fay prepared Milly to look sweet in a pretty floral gown to attend church with Jeb. Will and Brian decided to go as well and asked who would like to ride with them. Sarah decided to take the children and go, so only three women were left at home.

Locking the doors after everyone left Mariah and Fay would celebrate the Sabbath with a Bible reading, an interpretation and a couple of hymns. Tilly was invited to join them, and the smile on her face witnessed that she was happy to be included.

Before they began, Tilly had a confession. Looking at the other two she felt shy to share. "I can't remember when I ever had a day off work. Miss. Mariah and I want to thank you for being considerate." She looked down at her folded hands. "Don't know right what to do, never been to church, can't read, and only know to sing church songs by heart."

"We are all Gods children Tilly, so we help one another. Would you like to learn to read?"

"Am I not too old to learn?"

"You are never too old," Fay reassured. "We can teach her can't we Mariah?"

"Yes, we can, and Sunday would be a perfect time, let's have a church service. Fay and I can read and then you can choose the hymns you know Tilly."

The reading was from Galatians 5:22-23 "But the fruit of the Spirit is love, joy, peace, long-suffering, kindness, goodness, faithfulness, gentleness, self-control. Against such, there is no law."

Each woman took turns in giving their interpretation on what this meant. Tilly laughed that each word represented fruit.

Mariah didn't want to overload Tilly with teaching that

she would have difficulty understanding. So she asked, "Do you like fruit, Tilly?"

"That I do Miss. Mariah."

"Why do you like fruit, Tilly?"

"Why my mother said an apple a day is good for your health. All fruit is good for your body."

Mariah smiled. "So are the fruits of the spirit Tilly, If you love and are loved, then like eating fruit, you will feel happy and be glad of it. It's the same with all the other pieces of GOOD fruit. They nourish you and help you do things Gods way. The healthy way."

She could see Tilly mulling this over and knew that as she learned more of Gods Word, it would come together like a jigsaw puzzle in her mind.

Changing the subject Fay asked. "What Hymn shall we sing?"

"It is well with my soul," Tilly smiled.

They all sung together with Mariah needing to sing softly so as not to drown the other two. It was her first time to use her voice thus in a couple of weeks since leaving the Opera House. Tears sprung to her eyes as against her better judgment she suddenly missed the place.

Milly and Sarah arrived back from church thrilled with their experience. Jeb stayed for leftover lunch and then took Milly out for a drive. "Don't you go worrying about your aunt now, she'll have supper at my place, and I'll have her home soon after."

Mariah was happy to see the way her aunt flustered like a young girl. Perhaps the two should have been chaperoned, but truthfully, Mariah felt it was a silly old-fashioned idea and would say so if anyone dared to comment.

Sarah spoke of the service and the kind unmarried Pastor, Caleb Murray. "Not many people were there," she informed with a frown. "For the amount of folk living around here it was disappointing." Tommy nodded in agreement.

"I counted them on my fingers," he held his hand up proudly. "There were this many." He showed ten fingers and then another four.

"Really," Mariah frowned. She had an idea of how to fix that, but it would need to wait awhile.

Milly, Brian and Will all arrived home after supper, with Milly requesting her niece see her later in her room. Firstly, Will and Brian needed instructing what work Mariah wanted done the next day.

"I want the front grounds cleared and made to look respectable, and please keep that done weekly. I'll send one of you to the store to purchase whitewash; the outside of the house needs refreshing first, then later the inside."

"It's the kind of work we enjoy doing, don't we Brian?"

"Sure do, and we know about caring for the animals, no problems there."

Tilly was told to keep on with the kitchen care, cooking, looking after the small vegetable garden, and washing all clothes.

"If I see you are doing well, I will increase your wage by ten dollars more a month, and if you like, we can open a bank account for you to save."

"Oh, Miss. Mariah, you don't need to fret any; I'll do real good. I did never have a bank account."

"I'm sure you will be wonderful Tilly, Oh, and by the way, if anyone knocks on the door at night, you are not to open or to speak to them, that's very important. I don't care who they are. If you are unsure, then come and tell me."

"I understand Miss. It might be that no good Noah I don't want no more trouble from him."

"No, you don't Tilly. You will meet and marry someone

wonderful one day and have a happy life. Now good night to you, I'll see you in the morning."

*****

Milly waited for Mariah in the main bedroom full of how her day had panned out with Jeb. "He's a wonderful man you know. He told me that he is sixty-five, that's almost fifteen years more than me Mariah, but I like him."

"I know he likes you Aunt Milly, and he is youngish for his age let him keep on courting you and see where it leads. How was the church gathering by the way? Sarah tells me the congregation is weak."

"Oh, I felt sorry for Pastor Caleb, such a nice man, tall with reddish-blond hair and lovely eyes. He has such excellent manners too."

"That's good to hear."

"Yes, and I invited him to supper tomorrow night. I don't wish for him to starve. Perhaps we can give him milk and eggs to take home."

"Of course we can. I'll enjoy meeting this man of God. Well, let's say our prayers and go to sleep, tomorrow is another day."

*****

On Monday everyone got busy. While Will went to purchase the whitewash and brushes to paint, Brian got into clearing the weeds away. It was hard work, and Mariah insisted he eat his lunch and rest before continuing. When Will arrived back at home to help then Brian could continue. These two cousins were a good team and worked well together.

Will came home with the paint and pleased that he received a discount for buying so much at once.

Brian informed Will he had better work hard that afternoon as he was tuckered out. Mariah gave Brian a dark look when he walked in the door without brushing the dirt from his overalls and removing his boots. He understood immediately, hastening to rectify his fault.

They hoped to begin the outside house repairs by Wednesday. Tommy wanted to help the men, so he carried them water whenever they needed to drink. Little Rebel as she remained called, was placed outside on the front porch in a big box with some toys. She happily watched her brother or played while Sarah took charge of the house.

All the clearing work was coming together. Mariah stood on the front porch watching Will and Brian still mowing the grass after having used a scythe to get the longest down. The time neared five o'clock, and Mariah felt they'd worked enough for today. Tommy had taken his job as a water carrier seriously, now sitting on the front steps, he watched and waited to carry them a drink. This time was well spent playing with a grasshopper.

"Tommy, would you be a good boy and go tell the men to finish off? They can wash-up and rest before supper."

Tommy felt proud to have this responsibility and putting the insect in his pocket, ran to do her bidding.

Remembering the pastor was coming to visit Mariah went inside to remind the others. Rebel had just awoken from her afternoon nap smiling she reached her arms out for Mariah to pick her up.

Sarah looked on with a smile, "She is getting spoilt with everyone carrying her around. I think I'll bring that push toy horse downstairs with us to the dining room while I set the table. It gives her something to do, and she feels big to push it around."

Rebel still wore her boy clothes, and they gave her more playing freedom instead of tripping over long skirts.

The smell of food cooking filled the house, stirring hunger so that everyone was ready to eat as soon as placed on the table. Mariah went to see if the meal waited for serving on time. She found Tilly bending down to the oven removing one apple pie and then another. These were placed on the bench to cool before Tilly stood back to admire the golden brown crust. She looked at Mariah who nodded in approval; her mouth salivating at the thought of this served with clotted cream.

*****

Pastor Murray knocked on the front door at the expected hour. Tilly answered taking his hat and escorting him into the dining room where the family stood waiting. Sarah introduced him all around to everyone except Milly because she'd met him yesterday.

He seemed to hold Fay's hand longer than necessary with Fay blushing then casting her eyes down. Mariah had never seen her friend ever act like this. She sat him across the table from Fay, where from seated at the head of the table, Mariah could discreetly watch their interaction.

The pastor said grace before they began and it made Mariah realize they needed to keep doing this from now on. There was much to be thankful for and looking around the table at the happiness of each person Mariah was especially glad to see her aunt thriving.

"Young Tommy," Pastor looked next to him. "I am

wondering how you would feel about looking after a puppy for me?"

Tommy stopped eating full of interest. "What kind of puppy and what about its mamma."

"Yes, Hm that's something to consider, but his mother has another four little ones, three more boys and a girl. They are wearing her out." Pastor glanced up at Fay with a knowing smile.

Fay smiled back before she concentrated cutting up her food. Mariah hid her grin knowing Fay was impressed by the minister, and he with her.

"Well Sarah," Pastor addressed Tommy's mother. "Would, you be happy for Tommy to have his very own dog? It's mostly labrador by the look. His mother wandered in starving and ready to give birth five weeks back. I'd say by the end of this month Tommy could have the pup if you're willing."

Tommy's eyes pleaded with his mother to agree. "You'll have to ask Mariah, son."

"Can I please Aunt Mariah? I will take good care of him and feed him my leftovers."

Mariah looked at the boy knowing it would be good for him. "Of course you can Tommy because I know that you are a man of your word." Tommy swelled with pride and nodded to Pastor.

"Can I see them on Sunday?"

"Yes, sure you can, right after church."

"Might you be coming on Sunday Miss. Fay?"

Before Fay could make an excuse, Marah answered for her.

"She would love to Pastor, and before we get off the subject about those puppies, I would also like to have one. It would be good to have a warning bark when anyone is around."

Chapter Twelve

Milly's Special Moment

It would be seven weeks to the day before the night riders appeared again. Mariah had begun to think they wouldn't be back but Jeb shook his head and rejected her assumption.

He sat on the front verandah with Milly while enjoying a cigar. The evening stars shone in a clear sky predicting a further relief from the heavy rains of last week. Fairways was back to looking the presentable plantation it once was. New green shutters now sat either side of the downstairs windows ready to be functional in rough weather as well as decorative to the eye.

"They'll be back." He finally spoke to Mariah. "That load in the cellar is worth a mint; they are biding their time to get the best price, so don't go letting your guard down. There is a steamer coming in shortly that's bound for New York, and I wouldn't be surprised if it's intended to carry the goods."

Milly sat up in her chair turning towards Jeb with her hand on her chest. "Oh goodness, I don't like hearing this."

Jeb's hand went out to fold over her's. "Perhaps you ought to come home with me Milly."

"I couldn't do that, I'm a single woman, what are you suggesting Mr. Rigby-Carson." Her stunned expression looked mortified.

"Well, perhaps you need to be a married woman who is well protected by a loving husband then dear lady."

"Are you saying what I think you are dear Jeb?"

"Yes, my dear. I would very much like you to be my wife. Do you think you can put up with me?"

Mariah got up to make a hurried departure. "I'll leave you two alone, so good night, I'll see you later Aunt Milly."

The two lovers barely heard her. Jeb stood up and lent his hand to pull Milly up to join him. With both arms surrounding her, he looked down into her sweet moonlit face. "Well, Milly, what do you say, I would be a delighted man if you say yes, we still have many years in front of us."

Milly placed both of her hands on Jeb's arms as she gazed up at him. Her heart thumped with both happiness and fear while her beloved stood patiently waiting. Why should she fear? He was a decent man and would take good care of her.

"Yes Jeb, Oh yes." How could she not agree to marry this wonderful man? Without further hesitation, he bent his head and kissed her lips. It came unexpectedly for Milly who was used to the occasional light peck on the cheek.

Their kiss was full of a passionate and love that resonates between a man for his woman. Milly felt faint with shock at the awakening desire that stirred within. Jeb held her gently close to his heart understanding her naivety and treasuring her virtue.

"We'll go into town tomorrow and buy you the prettiest engagement ring Milly, would you like that? You can choose whatever one you fancy."

Milly couldn't believe this. When expecting to be single forever and then soon to be a married lady, it was dream reality.

"Thank you, Jeb, I have always heard that a ring picks the person, so we'll see which one picks me."

Jeb chuckled, this lady was still a child at heart. Taking her into his arms once more, he gave her a good-night kiss. "You best go inside now my girl, and I'll see you at ten tomorrow."

When Milly was safely inside Jeb hopped into his carriage and rode off away from the home. Moonlight showed him the way and leaving his vehicle in the shadow of a magnolia tree; he hopped out to walk quickly back towards the barn.

Almost there and he was held up by Clay one of his men. "It's only me Clay, and I'm glad to see you awake and watchful. I think we'll be having some action around here before long, so keep a low profile." He patted his man on the back, then turned to go.

Swinging around remembering something he lowered his voice even more. "How is Ben? And where is he?"

"I'm right here Boss; I sleep in the day, not at night."

"Good to see." Jeb grinned. "Anyone been around?"

"No, everything has been quiet, but I've got a feeling when they come it will be on a night, with moonlight like it is now."

Jeb nodded his agreement. "I believe you are right Ben. Tomorrow I want to inform two more men to return here with you until this is over. It might be an idea to bring some dynamite as well. You can place it safely away from the house but in strategic spots to catch them unaware. I believe I will hear it go off from my home as well."

Clay and Ben liked the idea of that. "We got you, Boss; it

sounds a good plan."

*****

Jeb and Milly's wedding was set for the 25^{th of} July, a
Saturday morning at Fairways. Pastor Caleb, as everyone
now called him was to officiate with a short service held
in the sitting room of Fairways. All in the immediate
household were attending with Hart, Jeb's son.

Milly wanted to wear her mother's wedding dress that
was kept especially for her. In perfect condition
wrapped in paper and placed in a trunk all it needed was
a good airing. Her mother's Chantilly lace grown fitted
Milly perfectly.

*****

As so it was on their wedding day when Jeb's eyes
watched her descending the stairs, they spoke more
pleasure in them than any words.

Sadly Mariah's parent could not be present at short

notice. They would have loved to see Milly married and happy. Mariah would write and tell them all about it tomorrow.

Milly requested Mariah sing one short song at the end while the marriage register was signed. Not having used her voice or practiced since Louisiana Mariah prayed she didn't croak.

Standing at the side of Fay playing the piano, Mariah's voice was perfect as she sang. "Be Thou my vision, oh Lord of my heart. Naught be all else to me, save that Thou art." Hart sank into the nearest seat; he had heard that voice about two years ago, and there was no mistaking now to whom it belonged.

Looking across at his father their eyes met. Hart raised his eyebrows in a question. His father shook his head in answer; he hadn't known who Mariah was either until now.

No one moved, all were held captive by the moment. As Mariah finished the last note, Milly leaned up to whisper in Jeb's ear. "Doesn't she sing beautifully Jeb? Like a bird."

Jeb patter the arm threaded through his and whispered back." Yes my dear, like a lark to be sure."

Milly's hand went to her mouth. "It's a secret Jeb I will tell you the whole story tomorrow."

Not one person voiced the knowledge to Mariah that they knew who she was. The fact that she'd kept it secret meant there was a good reason. None of them would divulge her trust they owed her their loyalty.

Hart came to her side and looked deeply into her eyes. Questioning, without asking. "That was beautiful, and much like a voice, I heard a couple of years back." Lifting her hand, he kissed it meaningly. "I hope I get to hear more some time."

The pastor came next. "Your voice would draw many people to church, perhaps one day you will honor us with your presence??

"There is a serious reason why I can't come for now Pastor Caleb, but believe me when I say this, I will come when I can."

Tilly, Will, and Brian began to bring in the food. They were to remain and enjoy the festivities with everyone. Caleb gave Fay a plate to make her food selections. Watching them, Mariah noted Fay had relaxed in his presence. Smiling to herself, Mariah was glad and hoped to see more of them enjoying one another's company.

Tommy sat on the bottom of the stairs an arm around both pups who were growing fast. They were his closest friends, and he could often be heard talking to them. The golden colored one he named Lucy while the black coated was scruffy.

The piano began playing again, and this time it was Caleb with Fay. Jeb took Milly in his arms and danced her around the floor. Hart came for Mariah, and Brian took Tilly while Will drew Sarah and they all waltz. Little Rebel's eyes began to close while seated on the lounge. She drifted down to lay peacefully within the cushions.

As the clock struck five, Jeb whispered in Milly's ear with a nod she went to take Mariah with her upstairs. Her niece helped her change from the wedding dress into travel clothes. As Mariah handed her, her bag Milly's eyes shone with unshed tears. "You came home, and everything at Fairways came alive. I love you so much, Mariah."

She and her new husband were to catch the Steamer to Jacksonville, and it would take two days to reach there. Milly looked forward to her first ever vacation.

Hart and Mariah were to deliver the honeymoon couple to their departure point, concerned with returning after dark Mariah left instructions with Will. "Lock up everything as soon as we are out of the house and don't open up again until you hear my voice at the front door. I don't care who it is."

Hart looked at Caleb, " I'll give you a lift home on our return Pastor."

Caleb beamed. "It will be my pleasure to keep the ladies

company until you get back, Hart."

*****

Hart was smiling with a conspiring look on his face as he drove the buggy down the drive and out onto the dirt road.

"What are you up to Mr. Carson, with that wicked gleam in your eyes? Don't think you'll put something over me." Mariah was trying to work out the way men thought.

Looking sideways, Hart wore his best innocent expression. "Why whatever do you mean my dear, we are escorting the newlyweds to catch their ride, aren't we?"

Mariah shook her head and gave up. Who could out-talk a lawyer? Not her!

Chapter 13

Hart declares himself

The Paddle-steamer bustled with freight loading and passengers welcomed aboard while tickets were taken and help given.

Milly stared in dismay, "So many people, and a heavy load of cargo are you sure the ship is safe Jeb?"

Sensitive to her concerns Jeb didn't want to laugh and make her feel naïve. "Well Milly my love, I have traveled this way many times and am are still alive. There is nothing to be afraid of because we trust in the Lord."

Milly's face relaxed with Jeb's rational explanation. "Yes Jeb, we do trust in the Lord."

With regained confidence, Milly watched as Jeb and Hart lifted down two heavy suitcases.

"I hope I made the right choice with my luggage Mariah;

we are going for ten days. But I'm a little nervous about how to be a wife." She looked at her niece for advice.

"Jeb is a good man, and he will take care of you, so trust him, Aunty, he will help you. You are going to bloom." Mariah kissed her; then they walked together to join the men at the gangplank.

Father and son hugged, then Jeb hugged Mariah before turning to escort his wife on board. Hart and Mariah waited and watched.

The crew checked that all was clear and safe. Then the whistle blew a long shrill sound, puffing out steam as the paddles began to turn and the boat drifted away from land. Darkness descended, and a full moon rose as they watched it sail off.

On the way home the only sound in the still night was that of horse hooves clip-clopping along the dusty roadway. It was the only sound before an owl hooted its eerie call. Mariah gave an involuntary shiver, remembering the night riders. Knowing they would appear again when least expected, like ghosts, mysterious and dangerous.

Pulling into the gateway to Fairways the horse drew to a holt and Hart lowered the reins. His arm came around Mariah's shoulder, and he pulled her closer until she rested against him.

"I think many of us realized who you were when you sang today, but my heart was captured by you the most." His hand touched her hair as Mariah sat still, wondering about what was to come next.

She had a special feeling for this man, experiencing no fear. Turning his head, he captured her lips with his in a gentle kiss. His eyes were looking at her shadowed face in the moonlight to glean how she reacted. She smiled and leaned forward prompting him for another.

"Oh, my dearest, you are the vision from my dreams. Listening to you sing in the New Orleans Opera House two years ago I fell in love and knew that no one would ever capture my desire like you."

She sat silently listening intrigued by his words.

"I came back to hear you every night for the week I remained in town. You cast a spell that kept on drawing me back. How could I imagine that one day, one night I'd sit here with you in my arms?"

Mariah lifted her hand to caress his handsome face. A strong ecstasy filled her being. Was this love? She felt it was and yet caution compelled her to pull away. "I think we better go, Hart; I don't want anyone at home to worry."

Reluctantly he agreed. Reaching down to recover the reins, he gave them a flick, clicking his tongue. The horse trotted slowly along the driveway, seeming to take his time to the front porch. Both sat silently in thought as the buggy pulled up.

Hart jumped swiftly down to the ground, walking around to lift Mariah, security to the safety of his encircled arms. "Do you feel for me the way I do for you? Can I come calling on you as a suitor?"

He waited for her reply.

She hesitated, remembering the one man in particular, who had hurt her. But was this fair to Hart? The only way to know how so was to give it a chance.

"Yes Hart you can, but I give no promises, and you need to understand that." Her reply came almost in a whisper, and he could tell she was unsure.

"A relationship is a serious commitment, so we'll take it slowly, and with mutual consent."

His response to her was what she hoped he would say.

He gave her a quick kiss, then gathered her hand in his, to walk up the front stairs.

*****

Long after he had gone, Mariah lay in her bed pondering. She thought about her initial impression of him on the train and how her heart almost stopped. Yes, she was attracted to him at first sight, and the memory brought a smile to her lips. Gently her fingers traced over her lips where they had joined with Harts — what a glorious feeling that was. The bonding between two souls. Still, that was no reason to allow herself to become irrational. No, she must be cautious.

Everyone missed Milly and her ingenuous countenance, especially Mariah who was sleeping alone again in her large bed. Tommy had many questions about where Aunt Milly had gone, and why. He listened carefully as his mother explained she was married to Jeb now and was to live with him.

"But doesn't Aunt Milly love us anymore?" He mouthed his lack of understanding.

"Of course she does, she will never stop loving us, but Jeb was alone in his big house and needed company. They will come and visit us, and we will visit them."

What his mother told him could later be heard related to Lucy and Scruffy. He was now the all-knowing grown-up as he spoke to them with the authority his mother used. He finished by saying, "now don't go asking any more silly questions."

Mariah stifled a smile as she walked past him up the stairs. Tommy needed something to divert his mind from thinking he'd lost someone he loved. Something to occupy his mind but what?

She'd look in the toy room to see if she got any bright idea's. With a small rubber ball found, Mariah excitedly ran down the stairs and out of the front door knowing the boys' curiosity would get the better of him. It quickly did, with him and the dogs hot on her heels.

Standing on the porch, Mariah gave a yell and threw the ball while Tommy watched in puzzlement. Lucy sank to sit at her feet but Scruffy raced off after the catch. Grabbing it in his mouth, he proudly returned, dropping it at Tommy's feet.

"What do you think Tommy? Isn't Scruffy clever, will you throw the ball to make Scruffy happy?"

Tommy looked from her to the ball then the expectant

dog. He threw as far as he could and took after Scruffy to try to get to it first. Now Lucy wanted to join in and it ended with the three, rolling in the grass while Tommy tried to get the ball from the slobbering dog's mouth. It was a battle of wills as to who would keep control.

What fun they had the boy couldn't stop laughing. When finally in control of the ball and throwing it again, Lucy caught on to the game and tried to out-beat Scruffy on the claim.

Mariah sat on the porch and watched until they returned puffed out and ready to relax in the shade.

"So Tommy, you will be able the train these two to fetch whatever you want, do you realize how helpful that could be?"

"No?"

"Well suppose you are out in the sun and want a drink, you could prepare a bucket with some water in it waiting and send one of the dogs to get it for you." She continued to feed his young mind on possibilities.

"What if you got lost, and you sent Scruffy to bring someone to find you?"

Tommy absorbed Mariah's words, and she knew he would be a busy, happy boy from then on.

The following Wednesday Hart and the sheriff arrive to tell Mariah a small unknown steamboat with Spanish sailors was docked and waiting. Could this be what they expected? Could these be smugglers? And were they connected to the night riders?

"Let's step outside for a little talk." The sheriff led the way.

Standing in a clearing and speaking quietly the sheriff informed about two extra men in the barn making four on watch every night. "They are well prepared and will catch those scallywags once and for all. Don't you to be concerned about anything Miss. Mariah?"

"I think I should have a backup plan for the other women and children, Sheriff, and I know what I'll do." She was thinking about the secret passageway. Her only problem was in how to keep Rebel quiet. Hopefully, she would remain asleep.

*****

Suspense built that night as all waited, the men in the barn while Mariah kept the women upstairs behind the locked door of her room, Tilly included.

She did not explain, other than to say she had heard there might be a problem that night, and she wanted them all to be together.

Mattresses lay placed onto the floor for sleeping. Fay and Mariah were to sleep in the big bed.

After some talking, all drifted off to sleep, Mariah as well as the others. She awoke in the early morning hours. A dream startled her. Was the bedroom door being broken down; her body jumped in terrified response.

Chapter 14

Would they be Safe?

All was dark and silent. Hopping out of bed, Mariah padded across the floor, careful not to make a noise. Standing to look down on the back of the house and across to the barn, all looked normal but was it. After standing and watching in anticipation, Mariah collected a chair to sit and keep a vigilance. She was wide awake now, and her eyes continued to sweep the area for any unusual movement.

She sang and prayed in her mind while keeping her eyes focussed below. As the sun rose over the horizon and the open bulky window curtains allowed the brilliant light to gain entry, those sleeping began to awake.

Tilly was first to open her eyes, looking around the large room to get her bearing. Seeing Mariah sitting at the window, she got up and came over.

"Well, looks like we are all well and fine Miss., Mariah."

"So it seems Tilly, my prediction was wrong. Well, another day and I think it's time for a nice cup of coffee what do you say? But we best get dressed first."

"I say I'm going to the water closet first, and then, get myself into day clothes." Tilly gave a cheery reply.

"Meet you down in the kitchen; I won't be far behind you."

Nothing was heard or seen of the men from the barn, had it all been a dream, it seems so. Everyone soon trooped into the dining room for breakfast. Tommy asked Mariah with his mouth full of oatmeal if they were sleeping in her room again?

"Tommy" his mother chided, "don't talk with food in your mouth!"

He looked like he might cry from the chastisement.

"I'm not sure, yet Tommy we will need to wait and see. But I'm sure Lucy and Scruffy will want you with them in the nursery."

"I could bring them into your room, Aunt Mariah."

"Yes, but, the nursery is where they know so they would feel homesick, and we don't want them sad do we?"

He nodded his head in agreement. "I never want to leave Fairways, Aunt Mariah, because I would get very sick."

Leaning over she ruffled his hair. "And I might get very sick if you did."

Nothing unusual happened that day or night and everyone, except for Mariah, slept comfortably. At four in the afternoon, Hart came by. Tilly answered the front door to his knock, taking his hat while he wandered into the sitting room where Mariah played the piano.

He leaned against the doorway watching her until she

looked up and saw him. A smile reached the corners of his mouth, and his dimple danced in appreciation as she walked towards him.

Hart's amazing light gray eyes looked her up and down, to flee back to her face with a look of wonderment that this woman might one day be his.

Gathering her close, he kissed her lips, then placed his mouth close to her ear to whisper. "Let's go for a walk."

They went out through the front door, winding way over to the side driveway to stand under the magnolia tree. His arm still encircling her waist he turned her towards him. For anyone watching, they were a couple sparking.

"I wanted to come yesterday as I knew you'd be wondering what happened with that steamer and the night riders,"

"Ghost riders, yes I did wonder. I fell asleep and woke up thinking they had invaded the house, but it was only a dream. Oh, Hart, I'll be thankful to have this over with and be able to live normally."

"I know my dearest. Well, that ship left after unloading tobacco. Perhaps whatever these riders do, it will be unpredictable."

Mariah nestled closer to him. She smelt cigar and lemon a clean male smell and not the claustrophobic one of some town men. He felt good, reliable, and protective. Looking up into his face, she questioned. "Will there still be four men in the barn at night?"

"Yes, there will. And I don't feel we have long to wait either. I've noticed some strangers wandering about town, mean looking characters. As for my secretary Dennis Wade perhaps we could set a trap through him. That way if he's involved, we'll get this problem over and done with."

"How? What do you plan to do?"

"Look, I'll be back for supper, but I think I'll go now and talk to the sheriff and see what he says and then tell you after we eat tonight."

"Alright Hart, I certainly want all of this behind us, see

what you can do."

He walked Mariah back to the house then drove off with a wave.

Tommy ran up to her still standing on the porch. "Isn't Uncle Hart staying for supper, where did he go."

Mariah's heart fell. Keeping a secret was hard yet necessary. "Yes he will be back Tommy; he just remembered some work he had to do." She hadn't lied. For once she wished this inquisitive boy didn't ask as many questions.

Will, working in the pasture with Brian looked over at her. They would both need to know, as they likely wondered.

"Stay here for a moment Tommy; I want you to take Will a note for me." She walked quickly inside to the sitting room. Seated at the desk, she wrote a simple message *Hart will instruct you both tonight.*

As she gave it to the young boy and watched as he ran

off to deliver it, she knew they would both understand what it meant.

Will read it, then tore it to pieces placing those in his pocket. With a wave to Mariah, all settled for Hart's return.

Going to her bedroom and kneeling to pray she needed assurance of Gods covering over them all.

Help us to do your will in this Lord; I praise and thank you for your protection thus far. Forgive me my weaknesses In Jesus name, Amen.

She couldn't think what to say. Was her faith weak? The dependency on the safety of all weighed heavily.

Still kneeling with eyes closed her helplessness cried out from within her soul.

"When you are weak, I am strong" These words came, from beyond herself and lifted her to stand and open her eyes.

There he was once more. That magnificent angel of God

surrounded by light and love.

"Fear thou not; for I am with thee: be not dismayed; for I am thy God: I will strengthen thee; yea, I will help thee; yea, I will uphold thee with the right hand of my righteousness."

Mariah remembered this verse from Isaiah and spoke aloud. "Forgive me Lord and thank you for your messenger angel. I had forgotten this with the confusion in my mind. I trust in you. Be thou my vision and help my unbelief.

The angel faded before her eyes, yet his peace and love remained. With a sigh, Mariah walked from her room, before long Hart would return, she knew that whatever the plan, all would end well.

Supper was still over an hour and a half off, and the tranquility surrounding Mariah gave her a need to sing to the Lord.

Heading to the piano her heart wanted to praise and glorify him. Sitting down the right hymn came into her mind. "Tis so sweet to trust in Jesus, just to rest upon his promise, just to take him at his word......." Mariah sang straight to heaven with all her heart. Her voice, heard by the cousins, Will and Brian who looked up from their work. Then looking at one another and with a nod, they walked towards the house. Young Tommy ran to go with them. By the time they arrived the hymn changed to, Blessed Assurance Jesus is mine. Sarah, Fay, and Tilly stood in the sitting room doorway as the men joined them to listen. All were spell-bound as the Holy Spirit in a bright glow, and beautiful perfume rested on each.

Hart arrived back an hour later bringing Caleb with him. Mariah was still singing, and her audience rested in the lounge or on chairs.

Tilly remembered supper as soon as she saw the men come in. No problems, a stew simmered on the stove, and she only had a couple of cornbread pones. Apple pie's rested on the kitchen table with clotted cream in the ice-cooler.

Sarah bustled into the kitchen to help. Collecting the tea trolley, cutlery, and dishes were piled on and pushed to the dining room.

Hart had gone over to the piano and leaning on an elbow close to Mariah he whispered. "Let's go outside and talk before we eat."

Mariah didn't waste time, eager to hear what the night rider plan was she had to hold herself to a walk instead of pulling him out on the run.

Chapter 15

Catching the Mysterious Riders

Under the magnolia tree, Mariah sat on a log while Hart stood close by her. "Tell me, what's decided?"

"I hope it doesn't upset you Mariah because you will be the bait."

"How so?" She wasn't too sure of this.

"It was Pastor's idea. Would you be open to sing at the church not this Saturday night, but the following one?"

"How will that help?"

"This is what we are thinking." He sat down beside her taking one hand in his to look the part of a courting pair for anyone watching.

"If we broadcast it to begin at seven thirty that night. Everyone will know you and the others won't be at home. Those riders involved will think they have a clear field. I'm sure they'll take the advantage to come here and relieve the cellar of its load."

Mariah's hand went to her mouth in thought. "Yes, well. However, if I'm going to sing then, it won't be free or only for a Free-Will offering. We can get the newspaper to announce it with a cost at fifty cents adults and two pennies for children. The church needs money, so we'll make it help them.

"Pastor wonders if you will sing one song on Sunday, to give a taste of what's to come. BUT, we don't want anyone to see who you are until the following week. What about you wear a veil?"

"Let's make it secretive; I'll use more than a veil, I have a cloak that belongs to my mother as a fancy dress disguise. The more mysterious, the more people will come." She chuckled.

"You are clever Mariah," he laughed as well. "You will turn this town on its head."

"Let's hope so. Now, on Sunday I will walk in from the back of the church after the first hymn. Then I'll take off straight home after so that no one gets the chance to guess who I am."

"I'll take you there and deliver you back home again, all together we shouldn't be gone more than half an hour."

He stood up preparing to return to the house. Holding his hand out to help her, he pulled her up close for a kiss before they walked back.

They came in the front door just as supper was dished out. The talking around the table stopped as everyone watched the two be seated.

*****

Sunday shone like the Shekinah Glory of the Lord. The sheriff, Pastor Caleb, and Hart busily spread the word among the town folk that something secret would occur in the church on Sunday. People carried this information onto others — stemming curiosity.

Hart would be at Fairways at nine o'clock to pick Mariah up and deliver her to the back church entry. Will and Brian remained at home closed in with the dogs in case of any problem.

When Mariah walked out of the house into Hart's view, he roared with laughter. She was covered from head to foot in the black cloak belonging to her mother. A black gown, black hat with a veil and black boots completed her incognito effect.

Hart extended his hand to help her climb into the buggy. The perfume she wore was not her usual; it also belonged to her mother.

Hart smiled a conspiring mischievous grin. "Well done, you'll have everyone fooled. I heard Sarah telling Tommy not to say a word. She didn't want him to call out your name."

"This is more nerve-racking than to sing at the Opera

House. The audience will be in closer proximity."

"You'll be fine." He clicked the reins to get going.

Mariah praised God in her mind as they rode the dusty dirt road with nothing and no-one in sight. Well, Sunday was the day of rest and even those not attending church, still kept a rest time. She was holding her hat in place for it not to blow away then glanced side-ways at Hart. Sensing the look he smiled. She admired his strong facial muscles and unusual eyes, then wandered to look at his firm hands. She felt safe in his company. Another praise worship to God.

The church came into view with more in attendance than usual, a good sign. Hart drove carefully to the back entrance, trying to be as quiet as possible. With the singing, hopefully, no-one heard them.

Hopping from the buggy, he assisted Mariah to alight, lifting her to the ground. Inside the backroom, Hart lifted her veil slightly and kissed her lips.

The singing inside stopped, and Pastor began to pray.

While heads were bowed and eyes closed, Mariah tiptoed out to stand near the pastor.

Fay was ready on the piano for when the congregation lifted their heads.

After the gasps of amazement, Fay began the accompaniment to "Just as I am without one plea but that thy blood was shed for me."

Mariah's voice soared to the roof-top, holding the listeners captivated.

Watching them from where she stood and seeing the intent listening, she knew it would be a packed house next Saturday night.

A smile curved Mariah's lips behind her veil as she finished. Everyone stood, clapping madly.

Pastor Caleb waited until the noise receded, then held up both of his hands for quiet.

"Did you enjoy hearing the world-renowned voice of our visitor?"

"YES! We did." All responded.

"Well let's bow our heads and pray that we will have a wonderful night listening to more of our guest's voice come next Saturday."

All obeyed with no dispute allowing Mariah to slip away. Only one person peeped, - young Tommy, who waved as she looked back.

Returning straight home, Mariah ran upstairs to remove the underlayers of her abundant clothing. Hart retreated to the kitchen to place the kettle on to heat for morning tea. He called Will and Brian to join them.

Tilly had gone with the women to church for her first time. She was pleased to have a new dress to wear and be included as one of the family.

The men had morning tea spread out and ready when Mariah drifted in.   "I felt stifled in that outfit. Considering we have now entered August, I would expect the weather to be cooling."

"It does what it wants to do, like all nature," replied Hart.

"I can recall it snowing, but perhaps that was later?"

"I'm glad we don't get what they do up north," Will looked up from drinking his coffee.

Brian let his cousin do the talking as usual yet questioned this. "What do you mean, we've never ventured north?"

"Don't need to go there to hear what people say."

*****

Hart was gone, and Mariah rested in her room when the others arrived home full of chattering laughter.

Fay was the one to seek her out in the bedroom. "We almost didn't have enough sandwiches. More folk came than expected. We sat around after the service and those who stayed shared our lunch." She withdrew her hat placing it in a chair before it followed with her shoes and then she plonked down on the bed beside Mariah.

Turning onto her side Fay's face was close to Mariah's ear. "Do you want to hear the talk that went around after church? Bet you do."

"Of course I do," Mariah closed her eyes while listening.

"Okay, this is what I overheard. Who is she? Her voice is divine. I can imagine she really is an opera singer. I'm not going to miss next Saturday night. Me either, I'm telling everyone. I can't wait to see her face. I bet she's beautiful. Why would she come to our town? Gosh, I never imagined the pastor would know someone famous. You can never tell a book from its cover."

Mariah's eyes remained closed. "It sounds like we stirred this town up."

"We sure did and perhaps after this Caleb will have a bigger congregation to hear, The Word."

"I'm sure he will Fay. Do you mind if I have a sleep, this

weather makes me tired."

"I think I will as well." Fay turned over on her other side and fell asleep almost immediately.

Chapter 16

The lure of a Voice

As Hart wandered through the town on Tuesday, he heard continual talk about the mysterious singer and the excitement for Saturday night to come.

Returning to his office, Dennis his secretary questioned him. Hart noticed the glint of excitement in the man's eyes. Testing to see how far he could be trusted, Hart asked if he would be going.

"No sir, I can't see that happening," Dennis looked away before adding. "Are you going to be there, sir?"

"I wouldn't miss it, and I'll be escorting Miss. Mariah there. All at Fairways plantation plan to go. We look forward to it."

Hart walked into his office leaving the door open to keep an eye on Dennis. The clerk seemed to find it hard to sit still. Then he got up from his desk and approached his boss.

"I know it's not a break time but its quiet so would you mind if I leave early?"

Hart thought to make Dennis sweat. "Where do you have to go that's so important, that it should interfere with work?"

He stood staring Dennis in the face making him nervous.

"I've never taken time off Mr. Carson, except for weekends that I don't work, anyway."

His eyes didn't meet those of his employer as he shifted from one leg to the other.

"You have only been here a couple of months Dennis, and we spoke on this when I took you on. Do you remember me stipulating no time off unless an illness or a matter of dire importance?"

" Yes, sir, I remember, and this is urgent to me."

"Okay, off you go then, but I hope it's not a regular occurrence."

Dennis raced off without a thank you or goodbye.

Walking to his office window, Hart could see him running down the street towards the telegraph office. He waited a while and then went to see the sheriff. They would both find out what that message contained and to whom.

Hart locked his office, placing a sign on the door that said CLOSED. He went into the Pharmacy to say he would be back tomorrow should anyone want him.

Then he walked to the Sheriff's Office to deliver his information.

"Let's go," Sheriff Taylor was as keen as Hart to learn what was so important.

The telegraph clerk wasn't going to argue with the sheriff and handed over the transcript. The message was simple.

THERE NEXT WEEK. Pooch.

The name of the receiver was Jasper Weaver of Tryon.

The sheriff scratched his head. "I reckon Dennis is telling this person he will get the delivery after they take it from the cellar. But we'll be ready for them." He removed his hat to wipe sweat away from his brow with a handkerchief.

"Do you want me with you Sheriff?"

They were walking down the street and speaking quietly.

"No, you go and listen to your girl sing. I'll have two deputies, and there are the other six men, plus dynamite. We can handle this."

Sheriff Taylor thought for a few minutes. "We need be careful how we go to Fairways; I don't believe we should all ride out there at once, anyone could be watching."

"How about the cousins ride into town that afternoon with the wagon? Then carry you three back out camouflaged and covered up with a few bags of flour or something."

"What about our horses?"

"Send them the day before with two of my father's men, looking like sellers."

"Okay, that sounds like it will work. The saddles can ride in the back of the wagon with us."

Times were worked out, and Hart could inform the men in the barn plus the cousins when he went to visit Mariah that evening. The plan was coming together nicely.

*****

Mariah wore one of her elaborate gowns on Saturday night. Fay helped her dress then with a towel around Mariah's shoulders she applied the heavy stage make-up. Lights were to shine on Mariah, with the audience kept in darkness. Adding this to the performance would provide a dramatic effect, keeping the audience spellbound.

Fay worked Mariah's hair into an artistic display with thin gold ribbon woven through the strands. She persuaded Mariah to hold a golden mask up in front of her eyes, then to reveal herself after the performance.

"It will be a mystery for them to wonder on until they find out."

Hart would deliver the women first with his father's carriage. Then he returned to collect Mariah's buggy and drive her there. As before, she was to enter by the back door when everyone was seated.

Pastor Caleb's voice rang out clearly from where she stood.

"The lady singing tonight is as I have said earlier, a famous Opera Prima Donna. She has sung here in America as well as Vienna, Paris, Rome, and London. We are very privileged for her to honor us with her presence. The money taken tonight goes to the church for some much needed renovating. I thank you all for coming to make the event successful."

When he finished, the lights came on at the front of the church and turned off at the back.

"We now welcome, The Golden Lark." With a sweep of his arm, Mariah entered and stood in front.

When the clapping stopped she curtsied, then Fay began to play, 'A bird in a gilded cage.'

Mariah put her heart into giving a professional performance with many songs to follow. Just before the supper break, she sang When Johnny comes marching home again.

Singing this sent the audience into a frenzy as it was one of their own songs. "More more," they chanted.

Mariah smiled and waited for calm.

Then in her best southern accent, "Thank you for your enthusiasm Ladies and Gentlemen. There are refreshments outside, and I will sing more on your return." With this, she walked to the back room.

A short time later Fay appeared with a tray carrying two glasses of lemonade and some small sandwiches.

Mariah patted the chair beside her for her friend to sit. "I'm enjoying this Fay. Back at my roots, and performing for people who would never otherwise get the chance to hear."

They looked over the next songs together. She would begin with the Hallelujah Chorus and finish with Nearer My God to Thee.

Mariah held her listeners captivated from the next song to her last.

At the finish, as the clapping receded, she removed the face mask. No one recognized her.

"Who here remembers Charles Segal?"

A few hands rose. "And what about John Kingsford?"

Many more hands rose as her father was a popular and well-liked gentleman.

"I am John and Francine Kingsford's daughter, Mariah. I left Swansboro when I was sixteen to continue training as a singer. Of late I sang as the Prima Donna at the New Orleans Opera House. For many years I have traveled the world singing in operettas. And now, here I am back at home and with you tonight."

She looked over at Pastor Caleb and nodded. He walked over to stand beside her.

"It's been a wonderful night." Turning to Mariah, he concluded. "We appreciate you lending your voice here tonight Miss. Mariah. And from all here, we invite you not to be a stranger."

Giving him a nod and a smile of thank you. Mariah gave a curtsy and walked out back.

Hart took her into his arms and kissed her passionately. "Let's go home; I still have to return here again for the others."

He looped her hand through his arm, leading her outside and down the steps into the quiet moonlit night.

Chapter 17

Caught by Surprise

Hooves thundered over the hill at the back of the plantation home. The leading rider held up a gloved hand signaling for all to stop. Looking over at Dennis he snarled, "are you sure there is no one around?"

"I watched them leave myself, boss. They all went to that thing on at the church as I told you."

Dennis and Noah sat close together on their mounts. They wanted to be a part of this gang; as it meant money and prestige. But if anything went wrong, they knew they'd pay, and that thought niggled at the pair of them.

Will was ready and alert at Mariah's bedroom window. Brian kept vigil in the kitchen with his rifle prepared. The dogs were gone so as not to make a noise. They were back with their siblings at Pastor's house, remaining until after church tomorrow,

It wasn't until safely under cover of darkness while the moon ducked behind clouds that two men crept out to strategically place the dynamite and prevent a getaway. With explosions and flashes of light, both horse and rider only had one route of escape, and that was where the sheriff and his men lay in wait, ready to corner them.

The two men who had been in the barn from the beginning remained there. They were the sharpshooter backups. Silently all eyes watched and waited, and they didn't have long.

One rider came in first likely as a decoy, then before long another and another followed until there were six. Behind them rattled a wagon with two more men.

There was not the usual performance of riding around the house and making noise. Likely because they suspected to be alone. Instead, they all hurried to work.

Two men ran down the outside cellar steps, throwing

their weight against the door. Cuss words drifted when it wouldn't budge. A stout set man still on his horse gave an order to break it down as he yelled at another to help them. Even then, the door wouldn't budge.

Like an angry bull, the boss man spun off his horse and almost fell in his rush down the stairs. "Good for nothin," he huffed, "I'll do it myself, get outta the way," he punched the man nearest to him.

Ranting and raving he threw himself against the barricaded door. "Someone has been up to mischief with my goods," he bellowed. "Wait until I get my hands on them."

A shot ran out from the barn to ignite dynamite. In quick succession three more sounded with a shattering explosion and fire, startling the riders into a frenzied panic.

One tried to flee back the way he'd come, yet before he raced past the barn, another stick of dynamite thundered, terrifying the horse who threw him. Laying on the ground unconscious, none of his friends willingly sacrificed themselves to help him.

The boss continued yelling orders, but none listened. They mounted as fast as possible tripping over their own feet in their stampede to break free. Only one way of escape looked possible. Little did they guess that the sheriff lay in wait, all ready to ambush.

Caught in the trap one man fired his gun and got shot off his horse in return.

During this confusion, the unconscious man who still lay on the ground was pulled to the barn and hog-tied. The cousins came in hot pursuit from inside the house to corner the angry Bossman and bring him down.

Noah tried to sneak away and was climbing the magnolia tree when caught by his pant leg and pulled back down. The deputy who captured him gave a stern warning not to try running again, or he'd be sorry.

By eight thirty all were securely tied and on the floor of the wagon for a rough ride back to town. Muttering and swearing, each blaming the other. These crooks struggled to get free, but freedom only happened when they were finally locked behind prison bars. And that wasn't the release they sort.

*****

Around ten o'clock that night Mariah and Hart drove in the gate and up to the house front. All appeared to be normal, Mariah saw nothing out of place. She looked at Hart with a query in her eyes.

He shook his head and shrugged his shoulders. "I have to get the others, and they'll be waiting, but I'll come straight back."

Mariah watched him drive away before knocking hard on the front door to alert Will and Brian.

Will opened the door after calling out to ask who it was. "Can't be too careful Miss. Mariah."

Mariah removed her hat to hang up before asking.

"Well, tell me what happened Will? Don't say they didn't come and we have to plan something like that again."

Her eyes searched his face for an answer.

"How about we go and sit down Miss. Mariah? I'll make us some tea and tell you the whole story and YES! They did come."

Mariah let out a sigh of relief, and Brian came through to the kitchen from his room. "Well it's over now Miss., and we can all sleep without fear."

Will turned from getting the kettle off the stove and poured boiling water into the teapot, then placing it on the table.

"Make yourself useful Brian and get the cups and sugar while I bring the milk. You like to gab away instead of helping."

Brian looked thrown off balance by the remark. "What's wrong with you Will, I have to hold the floor sometimes." He gave his cousin a friendly shove. "Sometimes it's my turn."

Mariah looked from one to the other; it was the first time she'd ever heard them have a word with each other. It was good to hear Brian voice his feelings.

"Hey, come here and sit down you two, and I want you both to take turns in telling me all about how you overcame those bady's. Right!"

Mariah poured the tea for all of them, then Will looked shamefully at Brian, "you go first, but let me tell about after we caught the bossman."

Over the next half an hour Mariah was filled in on every detail, and how good it felt to be able to breathe without the threat of lurking trouble.

A carriage was heard pulling up outside, and Will went to open the front door. Politely welcoming everyone home, he asked if they enjoyed the evening.

"Oh Will, Sarah's eyes shone." It was wonderful;

everyone mingled eating refreshments afterward, and many said they would be back for the service tomorrow. So I believe it was a huge success."

Tommy yawned and pulled on his mother's skirt.

"I know son, you're ready for bed, and this little girl needs putting down before she breaks my arms."

"Let me take her from you, Sarah. You lead the way for me." Will took the sleeping child gently into his arms looking tenderly down at her.

As they went upstairs, Tilly yawned a goodnight and hurried off. With only Fay, Will and Hart left they were ushered into the kitchen to hear the capture story.

Mariah got up, going to Hart and talking him by the hand, she led him back outside.

"Let's have some alone time, and you can tell me what you thought of my singing, and then I'll tell you about the success here tonight."

"First a kiss my girl, I've waited all evening thinking

about this."

They were over by the barn when Hart gathered her close and lovingly tasted her lips with his. With a groan, the kiss deepened with his heart hammering against her's.

"Oh Hart, you awaken a feeling of bliss that I never knew existed." The moon shone down on Mariah's face softened into an ethereal glow as she looked up at him.

"You have the same effect on me also my darling…… Come, let's sit over here and tell me how it went with those scoundrels tonight."

They strolled, enjoying the quiet, still air. Hart waited for Mariah to gather her skirts up a little before she sat and then he took his place beside her.

Turning to him, Mariah assured him he would hear the whole story.

"But first, the best part is, they are all in jail and will be for a long time."

Hart laughed, "we missed all the fun of it. However, beautiful lady, the night was perfection listening to your singing." He raised her hand to kiss the palm.

"And I enjoyed it as well. I think the church will see more people attending as of tomorrow. I have said that I will sing one solo every Sunday until before Christmas, and then we can have another performance of carols."

"Sounds good to me my dearest. Now, I want to hear the news about what happened here."

Chapter 18

Secrets shared

Following the Sunday service Pastor Caleb came back with them for lunch. With all seated at the table, Hart, with Mariah, described the capture of the night riders.

All the household were present including Tilly, who hearing about Noah looked up with the rest.

Brian placed his big hand over her's where it rested on the table. "No more worrying about him, Tilly, you are free."

"Are you sure Brian?" The look of uncertainty on her face spoke her fears.

"Yes, Mam, I sure am.. sentencing will commit all of those moonlighters right where they deserve, behind bars for a long time."

Tilly's hands covered her face as she burst out crying

from relief. "Free, no more Noah to bully me. I am an employed, honest person. Thank you, Lord."

Mariah passed her, her handkerchief with a smile. "Trust in the Lord with all thine heart, Tilly." Her gentle response acted as a soothing balm on Tilly's troubled soul.

"Well, that's one problem down and two more to go." Mariah looked over at Sarah. "I am going to share my predicament now Sarah, and I hope you will feel comfortable to share your one at some time."

Sarah looked uneasy. Tommy looked around at the grown-ups finding the discussion boring. Getting off his chair, then lifting his little sister down from her hers, he took her hand leading outside to the porch. His voice traveled to the rest. "You sit here Rebel, and I'll show you what good dogs I'm training."

Pastor Caleb turned slightly in his seat to watch the boy who was happy to have his pets returned. His attention roamed back to Mariah as she began her story of running away from Sir Thomas Whittiker. "I was glad the Opera season came to a close and looked forward to retiring and resting, but this man proved to be dangerous. So Fay and I made our escape and came back here."

Sarah's hand went up to cover her open mouth. Mariah looked like someone who had her life all together and now to hear her story was a complete surprise.

"I'm sharing this because we are all friends and can stand together helping each other. Secrets such as these although an embarrassment to the one suffering need to be out in the open with those they can trust. If a tall English man comes to town inquiring about me, you will know who he is and why he wants to know."

"Yes, and I'll give his name and description to the sheriff if need be," Hart reassured her. "But before that, I'll send a telegram to Judge Leon and find out the result of that court case. I'll need dates for that Mariah."

Mariah felt stronger having shared her load. Her eyes

settled on Hart now knowing he should have heard this before. "Gladly and hopefully, there will be good news from the judge."

Seeing the acceptance and considerate of Mariah's reason for returning home, Sarah decided she needed to be brave and tell her secret. Looking down and fiddling with a napkin while she shared her tale she was unaware of the shocked expressions passing from one listener to another.

Finally, Sarah raised her head. Fay, Mariah, and Tilly all wept at the thought of how Sarah had suffered. For a husband and father to inflict cruelty in the way described, upon his wife and small son, was unfathomable.

"I'll need names, dates and times off you also Sarah so that I can check on this monster. You should have reported him!"

"That's easier said than done Hart. I knew he had no feelings toward us and might have taken our lives. If I hadn't had the tad of money, my mother gave to me to keep for an emergency; we wouldn't have survived."

She gave a weak smile, "yes it's been hard, but then I met two angels who I will never be able to thank enough for helping."

Mariah reached over to hold Sarah's hand while Fay took her other. "We have all helped each other," Mariah assured.

"Yes," Fay agreed, "you and the children brighten, our lives." She looked to her side where Caleb silently watched the goodness of these women. Pouring himself a cup of milk he offered a scripture as support.

"The fear of the Lord tendeth to life: and he that hath it shall abide satisfied; he shall not be visited with evil."

"Thank you, Pastor Caleb, if it were not for the Lords leading I likely wouldn't be here." Sarah had a look of peace on her face that showed the truth of her words. She was secure in the knowledge that God did indeed protect. She began to help gather the dishes together in a heap. Standing, they were picked up and carried to the kitchen for washing.

Fay soon appear with more used dishes and cutlery. As Sarah poured hot water from the kettle into the sink and added a cake of soap Fay reached for an apron to cover her church clothes, keeping them protected.

*****

By the end of August, Hart had news for the two women, Mariah, and Sarah concerning Sir Thomas Whittiker and James Bowman. He came with the information one Friday evening remaining for supper and stayed seated at the dining table when finished.

"It took longer than I anticipated getting the information needed, Judge Leon was out of town and your husband Sarah couldn't be found. I hired a Pinkerton detective, in the end, to track him down."

Fay took the children upstairs so that young Tommy

couldn't hear about his father. Both children were content and happy, and there was no need for them to be otherwise.

Placing his wooden business case onto the table, Hart withdrew some papers. "Right, who wants to hear their news first?"

Mariah answered, "Sarah can be first so that she can see her children to bed." She looked across the table at the other woman who wore a terrified expression.

Hart also noted the dread Sarah displayed. "There is nothing to fear Sarah; it is all good news." He smiled at her then lifted a paper and read the Pinkerton report.

LET IT BE KNOWN

One Mr. James Bowman, a renown criminal of the law, left a trail of robbery and murder from Mississippi through to New Mexico. He was hunted down by Sheriff Lattimer and a posse. When he resisted arrest, he was shot dead in a gunfight between him and a Larry Oldman.

I witnessed the grave and can verify Mr. Bowman lies buried in the town of Hondo, New Mexico. No date is on his gave, only his name.

Very truly yours

Gavin Lawler

Senior acting Detective, with the Pinkerton National Detective Agency.

Dated this day 26th day of August 1902

Hart handed the letter over, together with a Death Certificate for the 15th August 1902.

Sarah's eyes shone with unshed tears. "I shouldn't say it, but knowing this is a relief." She shook her head as though it was a difficult concept to grasp. "He was a big strong man, and I believe he thought himself invincible. But, it finally caught up with him."

She got up slowly from the table and thanked Hart for

the information and for helping to place her mind at rest. With a goodnight to both, she left the room and could be heard walking up the stairs.

Mariah and Hart looked at each other without a word for a moment. Shortly Hart picked up another paper. "This is a telegram from Judge Leon, and it came today. You can read it yourself and keep it. Sir Thomas remained in jail for two weeks because every time he came before the judge, he disrupted the court."

Hart scraped his chair back, to stretch his tired body before continuing. "In the end, he paid a massive fine and booked his passage to return to his estate in England. Scotland Yard has confirmed that Sir Thomas is residing back in Birmingham, The Midlands."

Hart handed the lengthy telegram to Mariah. "I feel you have heard the last of that noble gentleman, as he swore never to return to the United States."

Silently Mariah read every word for herself. This information about Sir Thomas was excellent news, and she felt like shouting with glee, however, being a lady and understanding it to be unethical, she stood up, pulling on Harts' arm to do likewise. Then reaching both arms up to link around his neck Mariah pulled his face close to hers. It was the first time she took the initiative to kiss him, and she did so with every ounce of passion she possessed.

Hart groaned, encircling her waist with both arms to hold her tight. When they finally drew away and searched each other's face, a mutual love burned in both pair of eyes.

"You're going to have to make an honest man of me now after kissing me so completely." Hart winked at her.

Before Mariah had the chance to answer, Hart was down on one knee before her. "I love you, Mariah Kingsford. Would you do me the honor of becoming my wife?" His face spoke of love, and with a lock of hair falling over his forehead he looked too irresistible.

Mariah jumped up and down on the spot with

excitement, "Oh yes, of course, I will. Get up and kiss me again — goodness, my aunt with your father and now us. Our family has a vital bonding." Passion overtook as they embraced with enthusiasm holding on tightly and not wanting to part.

Chapter 19

A Cookout Gathering

Colonel Jeb and Milly were due back home in Swansboro the next day, and they were expected at Fairways for a cookout in the evening to celebrate. Hart suggested they keep their engagement a secret for the first half of the night and then surprise everyone with the announcement.

"Yes Hart, I like that idea, and it will be a fun surprise to all." Mariah laughed cheekily.

"I have my mother's engagement ring, Mariah; she hoped I would one day give it to the girl to whom I proposed. It's a large rare blue benitoite gemstone with tiny diamonds all around. I know many girls like to pick their special ring, so if you would rather, then we can take a day to go shopping."

Mariah thought this over. "It sounds lovely Hart, but I'd like to see it before making a choice, do you mind?" She inclined her head to see his facial expression.

"Not at all, and I completely agree. So, I'll bring it with me to show you tomorrow night." Gently he lifted her hand, kissing the palm while drowning her with his eyes. "I had better go. I don't want to, … you know that don't you?"

She smiled and nodded, the feeling was mutual. Running her fingers tenderly through Hart's hair then touching his beloved face, she whispered. "Go." It was all she could voice with the emotions playing like a stringed harp in her heart.

*****

Many of their new church friends came to attend the cookout bringing all kinds of preservatives and home cooking with them. Milly arrived looking like a modern woman on the arm of her husband. She wore a new dress and a changed hairstyle. Happiness glowed between the newlyweds as they greeted everyone.

The night was a huge success, and when one man produced a fiddle with another his harmonica, dancing and laughter rang out. Men drew their womenfolk up to twirl them around until both became breathless. Children ran around playing hide and seek with the two dogs, Lucy and Scruffy chased after them barking loudly.

Hart walked over to Mariah placing his arm around her possessively, knowing it drew interested attention. People watched as he led her among the dances to hold up a hand, commanding silence. Once all calmed Hart spoke with one arm around Mariah's waist, and the other feeling the ring, he'd soon place on his beloved's finger.

Mariah could hardly wait. She had seen the ring and fallen in love with its outstanding beauty. Hart still paused, looking around and waiting for the scene to be set with anticipation.

"We have an announcement. Mariah is going to sing. NO no, I'm joking." He laughed at the confused looks.

 "Tonight is the night that Mariah and I want you all to know, we are engaged to be married." Taking the ring out of his pocket Hart slipped it onto her finger, then turning her to face him, he kissed her.

Mariah held up her hand for all to see turning it in different directions for it to sparkle in the lamp glow.

"Let's not wait too long before we marry," he whispered in her ear as people surged forward to congratulate them. Jeb and Milly waited until last before coming to hug them both.

"Milly and I prayed for this to happen," Jeb informed them. "You are well suited together."

Milly flustered over Mariah's unique ring. "Where did you get it, it's so you?"

"Well Aunt Milly, your husband will answer that for you, but please wait until you get home to ask him." She hugged her aunt looking to where Jeb stood back smiling and watching them.

Fay and Sarah joined in the admiration. "When did you have the time to go shopping?" Fay questioned. "Fancy keeping it a secret from me." She gave a sad look and pretended to be hurt.

"But now your secrets are to be shared with the new and most important person in your life." Fay looked with approval at Mariah's choice. He was a handsome genuine man with a stable future. She would write to Mariah's parents Francine and John Kingsford tomorrow, informing them and knowing they would approve of Hart in every way.

Thinking on this and her own secret, Fay burst out laughing as Caleb drew close to her side nuzzling his nose intimately on the side of her face.

"You smell like a fresh rose."

Changing the subject, Fay whispered. "Will we tell them, Caleb?" She looked up at him for confirmation. Both she and the competent minister glowed looking into the eyes of the other while they seemed to be the only people in the world present. He laughed and hugged her.

"The time seems to be right, and I guess it would be a good idea," he nodded.

Now Mariah and Hart wondered what was about to come. They looked at each other and then at the other couple. When Caleb winked at Hart, he guessed and sighed with relief.

"You two are going to be married also aren't you."

Hart waited for the yes nod before reaching out a hand to shake Caleb's. "Well done buddy she is a wonderful woman."

"Yes, she is that," Caleb agreed. "But I'll need to do something about providing a home before the marriage date can be set. We'll likely need your father to perform the ceremony as a judge. There are no ministers besides me within miles."

"I'm sure you will have no problems getting his agreement." Hart gave the pastor an affectionate pat on his back.

Chapter 20

Exploring the Secret Tunnel

After lunch on Sunday as they walked and talked together outside and away from all the others, Mariah confided in Hart.

"It's been on my mind to share this with you, Hart, because it's been hard for me to keep such a secret for all these years." She stopped walking and pick one of the wild roses bringing it to her face to smell the perfume. Hart said nothing just stood waiting while Mariah worked out in her mind how to tell him.

"My grandfather always favored me, and when I was about fifteen, he took me into his confidence and told me something that none other than he knew." She brushed a stray hair back, tucking it behind her ear before continuing.

"Now I am older; I understand his reason for telling me about the tunnel. He wanted to know if I was trustworthy. He was a deviant of a man that wasn't genuine, and so, he didn't believe others were."

She stopped for a moment to see how Hart was responding. He patted her back fondly and nodded encouragingly, waiting for her to continue.

"Well, he took me down to the cellar one afternoon when I was the only family member at home. Pulling away a shelf from the back wall, he showed me a door and said it led through a tunnel out to the other side of the hill behind Fairways. He told of it being constructed during the Civil War, and he wanted me to know it was there, - just in case."

Mariah gave a puzzled frown. "His words of, just in case, are something I can't figure out, but then he said, to never go through the door or look inside or he would know. I was too frightened to go anyway and not knowing what would happen if I did, stopped my curiosity."

"Have you told anyone else about this tunnel Mariah?"

She shook her head. "No, I haven't, and I still haven't looked inside."

Hart took her hand, leading her back to the house. "There is no time like the present with the two of us together. But we'll need lanterns. Do you still want to keep it a secret from everyone?"

She stopped walking to look at him. "Why Hart?"

"Well, I feel it would be better to take say, the cousins with us. They have proved trustworthy, and they know more than us about the hazards of being underground."

"You're right, let's go and see what they are doing." Picking up the front of her skirt and with excitement flowing she could hardly wait.

*****

Will and Brian were more than happy to be included in the confidence.

Mariah felt it wise to let Fay know where they were going just in case of a catastrophe happening. Fay was visibly upset to know Mariah would be down there with the men.

After changing into a shirt, pants, and boots, Mariah felt she could manage well.

Will was to take the lead with Brian bringing up the rear. On starting, each carried a lamp as they stepped into the dark, dank smelling tunnel.

Mariah grabbed Hart's arm who'd insisted he be in front of her. She followed close behind him holding up her light to one side of the wall.

Will gave a whistle that echoed far beyond into the unknown darkness. Talking to those behind him, he informed. "The walls are beginning to widen folks, and I must add, this place was built to last forever. Look at the strong structure and how well it supports the ceiling." He lifted his lamp to read some writing on the wall.

"He who walks within these walls and doesn't belong, won't remain. Soon he will be gone."

"Well, that's short and to the point, but it looks like an old statement so no need for fear. I hope there aren't surprises in waiting to shock us." He trudged on slowly and carefully with the others on alert from behind.

Something touched Mariah's face and began to scale across it. With a scream, she dropped her light falling to stop on a slant beside the wall. Mariah jumped around, slapping at her face unsure where or what it was. Hart quickly rescued the lamp before it damaged and sighting an enormous spider on Mariah's hair he knocked it down and stamped on it.

"It's gone, and was not a dangerous one, just frightening."

"Oh Hart, I hate spiders." She sagged against him, her heart pounding and feeling weak at the knees.

Will was still walking.

"Looks like a room here to the left, there's an old wire bed you can sit on Mariah." Holding the lamp above his head Will now sighted more than a bed. A figure lurked in the shadows looking like an apparition. On closer examination by Brian, it turned out to be a skeleton dressed in rotting clothing and leaning against the wall. This could mean only one thing. Whoever it was had died in here and remained until now. "I wonder who he was." Hart stepped closer while Mariah sat on the edge of the bed. Feeling carefully inside the strangers pockets nothing of interest was found other than a neatly wrapped piece of newspaper.

Opening this Hart read the following.

LIQUOR LAW ENFORCEMENT OPPOSSED
September 14, 1868

Beware, illicit distillers. The Bureau of Revenue has established an Internal liquor tax to all distilleries. The town's middle-class highlanders who embraced temperance, have agreed that they will no longer stand for the mountain residences living in west Northern Carolina distilling and drinking alcohol. A certain gentleman by the name of Charles Alfred Segal who plans to reside here has approached those of the democrat and republican parties seeking support against these taxes. Many residences from the town and mountains are opposing each other over this situation. Please keep the peace.

Hart looked up from what he had read, "well we all know the crimes committed back then, and it looks like your grandfather was somewhat involved in this Mariah." He turned the piece of Newspaper over, but nothing of importance showed on that side.

"Well, I wonder what this had to do with this man's death? Perhaps he was a revenue agent who stumbled upon something he shouldn't." Hart put the paper in his pocket. "I'll search to see if anyone was reported missing around these parts some twenty to thirty years ago. It's a long shot, but perhaps a family somewhere lost a loved one."

"What will we do with this body Hart, we can't just leave it here?"

"We'll have to, for now, Will, until I can find out if there is someone to claim it. If he was a government agent, then they are responsible for his burial."

Hearing this distressed Mariah, she began to wonder if her home and land accumulated from the misfortune of others. She had a sick feeling in the pit of her stomach that it had been and questioned in her mind, how to amend it.

Will removed his pocket watch to see the time. "It's almost four o'clock, we best keep looking, or we won't be back for supper."

Out into the tunnel again the excitement at the beginning of this adventure was now gone for Mariah and replaced with a deep sense of regret.

Slowly as before, in single file, they walked another hundred yards or more discovering a large room at the end. No outside light entered, but the lamplight showed box upon box containing contraband piled high.

By the state of thick dust and spider webs, these had survived many years without discovery. "More

Moonshine by the looks," murmured Brian scratching his head. Will and Hart nodded in agreement.

"Well we have to leave this for the authorities, so let's continue and see how to get out of here."

Hart took Mariah's hand, noting the shocked look on her face. Drawing her close and kissing her forehead he whispered, "We'll try to do what we can to put this wrong to right. God knows our hearts Mariah, and he will find a way for us to do it."

Will and Brian were going towards the other side of the room to find the way out. Not walking far before the track looped around, then led outside. If anyone had seen the cave, it would have looked inconspicuous. Boulders on either side and above cleverly gave a firm foundation for the opening. Hidden in the corner of the hill where rocks and brush abound all over it gave no hint of suspicious or illegal acts well hidden.

"Ingenious," Will proclaimed. "No one would find this entrance unless they knew where it was. I doubt we will find it again unless we leave a marker nearby."

"You men all turn your backs, and I'll get what you want." Mariah pulled the shirt out from her pant waist and tore off the tail. It was long enough to tie on the branch of a nearby dead tree and sufficient to help find the entrance again.

None wanted to return through the tunnel, they have seen enough, and it was easier to climb the hill and head down to the plantation house in the fresh open air.

"Thank you, Will and Brian, for coming with us today; there is no need to suggest you keep what we discovered among ourselves as I know we can rely on your diplomacy."

"You sure can Mam," Will answered, "there is no way we would jeopardize our job here."

Mariah could not have felt more secure than with these three decent men. Will looked at his fob watch once more. "It's another hour until supper, so I think I'll get me a bath. How about you Brian if I know you want one also then I won't take as long?"

Brian turned his head and jokingly sniff under his arms. "I reckon I do if I don't wish to offend the ladies." Will pulled Brian's hat down over his eyes and took off running. Brian laughed good-naturedly. "He thinks he has a chance with Sarah and wants to spruce up." Mariah and Hart looked at each other and laughed as well. It seemed romance was thriving around Fairways.

Chapter 21

Finding the Truth

Hart got busy first thing Monday to see if he could find out who belonged to the cave skeleton. No longer having a secretary since losing Dennis along with the night riders, he waited for a replacement since advertising through the local paper.

Going to The Tideland News office, Hart requested their earliest editions to hunt through hoping to find information about any missing persons.

Sitting at a small table, with head his down Hart slowly scrutinized each page, yet finding nothing. Looking up, in thought he saw the editor was surveying him.

 "What is it Hart, what are you looking for?"

"Well, Ralph I was hoping to find out if anyone went missing around this area back twenty or so years ago?"

"That's a long time Hart, leave it with me. My father-in-law has a good memory, I'll ask him tonight. Someone you knew?"

"Well, you know my business is highly confidential Ralph, so I'm not permitted to say." Getting up from the table and shuffling the newspapers together, Hart placed them on the counter glad to give a reason for not explaining.

"I'll be back tomorrow, and hopefully you will have some information." He dipped his hat and headed out of the door. Next stop was Sheriff Taylor's office, and Hart hoped he'd be there.

"Well Hart, to what do I owe the honor of your pleasure this time?" Don shook his hand as soon as Hart entered.

"Another problem I'm afraid Don."

"Well, let's go sit in my office, and you can tell me."

As soon as they sat with the door closed on listening ears, Hart informed him about the tunnel and what they'd found.

The sheriff scratched his head. "Well! What a dooly. The government is not going to like the fact they missed finding all that contraband I can tell you. Unlike the other find that was recent. How many others know about it?"

"Just the four of us who went looking." Hart leaned his chair back on two wooden legs. It sounded like there would be a problem and not one that a Christian woman like Mariah would want to be shared.

"Look, this has nothing to do with Mariah or anyone else at the Plantation. Her grandfather would have been responsible, and as he is no longer around, something must be worked out."

The sheriff held up both hands. "I know, I understand the predicament completely, but this needs handling with delicacy." Getting up the sheriff motioned for Hart to leave the office in front of him. "I have a government friend who may be able to give us the right advice; I'll contact him immediately and see what he says. It will probably be a week or more before I get back to you, but that tunnel's not going any place."

"Fair enough, we will wait, and meanwhile, I hope to find out about the other thing I mentioned." The sheriff nodded, shook Hart's hand, then turned to retreat to his office.

In deep thought, Hart kicked a stone out of the way with his boot. His mindset fixed on Mariah, her beautiful face and the mouth he loved to kiss. It brought a smile to his lips knowing he'd won her hand and hoped her parents would approve of him. Surely if this latest mess about the tunnel was worked out without publicity, it would help to win them over.

Reaching the door to his office, and inserting the key, a voice from behind called his name. Hart turned, without recognition of the young woman who stood shyly, looking at him.

"Well, and who might you be," Hart smiled kindly.

"My name is Elizabeth Miller; I am Chad Millars eldest. I've come about the job advertised."

Hart took in her appearance. Although young, she was clean, tidy, and eager so perhaps he could train her. He knew the family needed the money, so he invited her upstairs.

"Right Elizabeth I take it you know how to read and write."

"Yes, Sir and my family call me Beth. I can also type some, as the teacher at my school gave us girls lessons."

"Well, you can type, that certainly is excellent news." Hart invited her to sit behind the desk. He showed her a typewritten note on the wall that listed her duties.

"At times when I go out I would like you to keep the door locked as it might not be safe for a young girl to be here alone. You will still be able to type and do anything else needed doing."

The work hours were agreed upon as well as the weekly wage. "I will give you a months trial to see if you work out," Hart explained.

"Thank you, Sir, I hope I meet all of your expectations." She took off her coat and hat hanging them on a wall hook.

"Can I make you a cup of coffee Sir?"

"You can make us both one." He smiled at her taking the initiative as it was a good sign.

The next morning before work Hart went to see the Newspaper Editor. The bell of the door rang as he entered bringing Ralph out from behind his printing machine.

"Morning Hart, well there's not much to tell. My father-in-law remembered back in the '70s and '80s there was a lot of controversy regarding making moonshine and agents were often around making unexpected visits. A few went missing too, and so did some moonshiners. I was a rough time, and folks knew to mind their business and keep quiet for safety sake."

"Does that mean there were no checks on those who disappeared?"

"That's right Hart!"

"Many thanks, Ralph I can't do more than that can I?"

"Guess not Hart." He was already turning back to the printer not wanting to discuss any longer.

Young Beth stood at the downstairs door waiting to enter. She stood aside for him to unlock the door. "You look worried Mr. Carson, can I help in any way?"

"I believe a cup of coffee will fix it, Beth, and then we'll get down to work."

Hart sat at his desk staring out of the window down on the street below. Beth brought his coffee setting it down on the table before him. Seeing him still pondering over something, she told him. "If you need to know anything about this town Sir, my teacher Miss. Hogan knows just about everything. She has kept journals with newspaper clippings from as far away as the city of Charlotte. It's her hobby you see. She loves history and felt that this area would lose it if no one bothered to collect as much as they could."

Hart brightened, this was good news indeed. "Thank you, Beth; I believe I will have to visit your Miss. Hogan, perhaps we'll leave an hour earlier today so that you can introduce me."

Beth glowed with happiness to be able to help her intelligent employer.

Chapter 22

Who is the Skeleton?

At four that afternoon Hart left the office accompanied by his new secretary. The schoolhouse and teachers residence was on Beth's way home, so it was no inconvenience for her to go with him. She felt proud to be walking beside her employer.

Miss. Hogan looked the typical school teacher, with gray hair rolled into a bun, gold wire-rimmed glasses and a simple mode of dress. She smiled when seeing her old student walk in the door.

Looking from Beth to the tall well dress gentleman at her side, Hart could see suspicion in the teacher's eyes. He knew what she was thinking, afraid that Beth was being misled, by an experienced older man.

Before Beth could introduce him, Hart took the initiative stepping forward to shake the teacher's hand and explaining who he was. Miss. Hohan notably relaxed and breathed a sigh of relief. Before telling her the reason for his visit, Beth was permitted to leave and go home.

Hart took a deep breath looking around to be sure they were alone. Miss. Hogan stood in suspense as she waited, wondering what this was all about. Hart motioned for her to sit before he sat down.

"I hope to keep this entirely confidential," he began in a low voice.

"I understand Mr. Carson." She looked mortified at his implication that she was capable of betraying his trust.

He proceeded to tell her that a body found could be a male person who went missing many years before. He asked if she knew of any such persons, saying the sheriff would follow up on any leads. "But first Miss. Hogan, can you help us?"

The teacher looked cautious. "why are you asking me? people, around these parts, don't like informers and I don't wish to be known as one."

For a moment Hart despaired of learning anything knowing how closed mouthed these country folk always were.

"Miss. Hogan, no one will ever know what you tell me. Beth, for instance, thinks I am interested in the history of these parts. And that's all anyone needs to know. Any investigations will probably be away from this town."

The teacher considered what was said, giving it thought and hesitating whether to share or not.

Hart tried again. "Can you imagine one of your family disappearing and you never knew what happened to them. As well as that, not having a grave to visit, that's cruel Miss. Hogan."

"Yes, I see, and it would be very hard."

She removed her glasses and rubbed her eyes. "I recollect there have been a few that have gone missing about these parts. I'll get back to you in a day or so with names and dates you can follow. Need I say though, I know nothing about this if questioned."

Hart arose and shook her hand with thanks. "I will keep it to myself and not even tell the sheriff where I got my information. Thank you very much for your help, Miss. Hogan."

He walked to the door before turning. "And Beth looks to be a perfect help in her work for me. Congratulations on your excellent teaching."

His words brought a smile and blush, "thank you, Mr. Carson, that's good to hear."

Hart walked down the school room steps praying that the teacher would find the useful information he needed. He felt happy and confident that a name would be found for the skeleton, helping to put it respectfully to rest.

On Wednesday morning as he opened the downstairs

office door, an envelope slipped under the door was found on the floor. With Beth directly behind him, Hart picked it up putting it into his pocket. Up the stairs and into the reception room, Beth removed her hat and coat to hang them up before heading off to make their coffee.

Knowing Beth would take fifteen minutes to heat water and make the drinks Hart walked into his office and sat at the desk while opening his envelope. As expected it was from Miss. Hogan with neatly printed names on a piece of plain paper. Hart understood the pains taken for no one to recognize her handwriting.

Four names appeared. The first name could be ruled out as it was ten years ago. The other three contained useful information.

1881 Terrance Bell 37 years old, 6' 2" tall, brown hair, hazel eyes.

1882 George Davis 42 years old, 5' 11" tall, dark hair, brown eyes.

1882 Calvin White, 5' 8" tall, sandy hair, brown eyes.

Hart's height was 6' 2," and that skeleton was much shorter than him when he stood in front of it. He felt that it was likely Calvin White's height but how would he find out more about this man?

Beth could be heard returning with their coffee. Hart slipped the envelope into his pocket, then put his hand out to take the cup and saucer from Beth.

"This smells good Beth. Take your time and enjoy it. When you finish I need you to run an errand for me."

Hart sat down at his desk again, placing his drink to the side while writing a note to the sheriff. He gave Calvin Whites description and asked if he knew anything about him. If so, could the sheriff come to the office when convenient? Sealing the envelope and with the sheriffs name written on front he put it to the side for Beth, while picking up his coffee again. Under his breath, he voiced a prayer that the sheriff would know something to help.

It was the afternoon before Sheriff Taylor came to see Hart. He waited until Hart finished with a client before going into the office and closing the door.

Hart rose from his seat to shake Don's hand before sitting again. Both men spoke quietly with Don asking how he came to ask about Calvin White?

"You know I have my ways, Don, just as you have yours. I can't break trust and tell you who it was otherwise I may never receive information again. So, can you tell me anything about this person?"

"Yes, I can. Calvin came into town looking for work, and hired by Charles Segal. Later he was reported missing by Mr. Segal's foreman with nothing more ever heard of him." Don removed his hat and scratched his head, "strange business it was. Calvin White's father came looking for him, saying he had received a telegram from his son saying he was signing on as crew with a paddle steamer. I followed the information up at the time, but found nothing."

Tapping his fingers on the desktop, the sheriff shook his head in disbelief. "I was a young fellow then, and it was the first case I checked on, so I remember it well. The strange thing was that Calvin wore a built-up shoe because he had one leg shorter than the other. I couldn't imagine him working on a moving boat, could you? Did you happen to notice the shoes?"

Such a specific piece of knowledge, and Hart knew he wanted to find out as soon as possible. "Listen, I don't want Beth wondering where we are going so if you can wait half an hour, I'll be closing here, then we can check it out together."

"Sounds good to me Hart. I'll meet you at my office when you get through here."

Beth was busy finishing typing a couple of letters as the sheriff left. She took them straight into Hart for signing.

He read them through then signed them. "Good job Beth now let's call it a day. I'd like you to post these off for me, and then you can go home."

"Gee thanks Mr. Carson, ten minutes early."

"Sometimes I might have to keep you back ten minutes late Beth; it depends on the workload." Taking a coin from his pocket, he handed it over to her. "Buy yourself some ice cream to have on the way home."

Nodding her head, thanks, Beth took the letters and went to gather her clothing. She loved her job and praised her boss to everyone.

Chapter 23

Confirmation

Hart and the sheriff looked at each other in silence. They had found the built-up shoe and now knew this to belong to Calvin White. He hadn't gone missing at all. Instead, he'd met with foul play, and more than likely Charles Segal and his foreman were responsible.

"I'd rather Mariah doesn't hear about this, and I don't want anyone else knowing about this cave. How do you think we can get the skeleton out of here without it breaking up?"

Sheriff Taylor whipped an old blanket off the bed and lay it on the ground.

"Okay, I'll hold the top part, and you can get the legs, careful now, we'll ease it down." Holding the skull and as much as the top section as he could with Hart carefully dealing with the pelvis and legs, they got it onto the blanket.

Hart grabbed a rope tossing it on the blanket as well. Picking up two corners each they slowly walked out of the tunnel. Once back at Sheriff Taylors wagon the remains were lifted, with the blanket wrapped securely around and then tied.

"You coming back with me or walking over the hill to your sweetheart?"

"There will be questions if I do that. No, I'll return with you and help to get this gentleman to the undertaker. I hope you can find and inform his family."

It was a silent ride back with only the sound of horse hooves on the dirt road, and an occasional bird cry.

Is this what life was all about? a young man wanting to work and likely taken advantage of by his employer and then murdered? Who knows what happened to him? Hart pondered on this and the unfairness.

The undertaker's sat on the edge of town not far from

the cemetery. The owner, himself bone thin and dressed in a black suit which hung on him looked like one of his dearly departed. His face was bleak and morbid. He asked no questions about his new arrival, just showed Don and Hart where to place their bundle still wrapped in the blanket.

"I'll let you know in time what we are to do with this body Joseph. For now, keep him safe."

"You can count on me, Sheriff. Have you a name?"

"I have but until I find relatives, that will remain unknown."

Nodding goodbye to the undertaker, Hart and Don went back to the wagon where Don quickly pulled himself onto the seat.

"I'll get onto this tomorrow morning after a good nights sleep Hart. Finding Calvin after all of these years has shaken me. I always wondered where he was."

"Fine, and I can understand your feelings. It will be good

to put his bones to rest."

Hart tipped his hat while saying goodbye and walked over to the Livery stable to pick up his horse and carriage.

That evening after returning from Mariah, Hart sat on the back porch of his home with his father. Whispering so as not to alarm Milly he related the story.

Jeb passed his son a cigar and lit one himself before giving his opinion. "That old deviate, Segal, he has much to answer the Lord about. No one trusted him, yet he got away without ever being accountable. To think he is my deceased father-in-law. Thankfully his daughters aren't like him."

"What about all the moonshine Pa, I'll be glad when that's all gone? Can you imagine if anyone dishonest got wind of it being there?"

"Yes son," Jeb looked around making sure Milly wasn't within hearing. "That is a problem and one that I doubt the authorities will want to know about."

"Why is that Sir?" Hart leaned towards his father, resting his elbows on his knees.

"Hart, they don't want it known they slipped up by not finding that liqueur. All the problems from back then are long buried. No, they'll look fools instead of heroes if the truth gets out."

"What will we do with it then?"

"I'd say sell it. Goodness knows how it came to be, but it's silly not to sell it and help someone who needs the money." Jeb seemed to have an idea. "I remember hearing something about it used in cough medicine, now that's a worthwhile need."

"Okay Pa, well it's food for thought. Now I need to go and hear what Don Taylor found out from his government friend. Thanks for listening, and for your advice."

"Anytime, well I better go find my wife. Goodnight, son, it will all work out somehow." Stubbing his cigar, and then throwing it away, Jeb got up. He replaced his chair against the wall and strolled inside.

Hart remained seated looking up at the starry night. Sometimes he felt the weight of problems was overwhelming. But then he wasn't God, and he knew to give it over in prayer. "Lord, I don't know how to voice the exact need about this. I don't want anyone to feel the shame of what another has committed. Help me to make the right choices for all concerned. In Jesus name, Amen."

Hart felt his prayer insufficient, yet God as his Father knew his heart, and since his word said to bring all to Him, Hart was satisfied he obeyed.

*****

To be fair to Mariah, Hart spoke with her the next night about their wedding. "Have you heard from your parents? When will they be here?"

"That's funny you should ask, we heard today. My parents are thrilled for us and can't wait to meet you. If all goes well, they will be here by the end of October."

Harts' face broke out in a smile. That was six weeks, so hopefully, the other sordid mess would be over with by then.

He placed his arm around her shoulders as she sat beside him. "Perhaps we could arrange to marry on Saturday a week after they arrive." He got up and walked to look at the calendar. "The end of October that's the thirty-first, so if we were to make our wedding day the eighth of November, there would be plenty of time. What do you say, Mariah?"

She nodded her head. "That's plenty of time to have a dress made. Will we be married here Hart or at the church?"

"If we have it here, then the supper could easily follow. Are you happy with that my dearest?"

"I am, delighted with that. As long as we have wedding photos taken with all the family at the front of the house, it will be faultless."

Hart pulled Mariah off the chair and into his arms,

holding her close. Snuggling her head into his neck, it felt good to have this man to help work out the wedding arrangements. Once married she would never be against the world on her own ever again.

Chapter 24

Making a Deal

On a Monday in mid-October, Calvin White's father and brother arrive to claim his remains. Mr. White senior was a fragile-looking man in his late seventies, with his son Lawrence likely in his early fifties. They came in a wagon living some thirty miles distance away. Sheriff Taylor needed a signature and date to say that Calvin White's family were claiming the body and taking him home for burial.

Hart performed the legal preliminaries. He assisted without any compensation because of the sad circumstances. There was nothing to be said to make it easier on Calvin's folks, although both the sheriff and Hart felt no need to mention about murder.

Both men stood watching silently with respect as the wagon drive off before disappearing around the bend of the road.

"Well, that's that," was all Don said.

"I have more news for you, Hart, if you come into my office." Don walked ahead opening the door for Hart to pass through. He took an envelope off his desk and handed it over. "You need to read this."

It was a letter in reply about the moonshine and said, the department knew nothing about anything from that long ago. The owners were informed to get rid of it any way they wanted.

Hart shook his head in disbelief. "Can you believe this? Rather than they take the responsibility, they are refusing to acknowledge it."

"That's about the sum of it, and what I expected."

"Yes, my father told me the same thing. They don't wish to acknowledge their incompetence."

"Well, I'll leave it with you, Hart. We did the honest thing and let them know, and now it's legal to keep it. Best save this letter as proof in case of any query."

With it in his pocket, Hart walked the short distance

back to his office. Although he'd locked the door downstairs before leaving, he wanted to be sure Beth was alright on her own before he did anything else.

The young woman was busy, typing away just as she had been when he left.

"I have one more errand Beth, but I don't like leaving you here alone. Do you have a dog at home?"

"Yes Sir, we have three dogs, why?"

"I'd feel happier if you had one here for safety, just in case. Can you bring it with you tomorrow? One that will be okay with my clients but will protect you if need be."

"That would be Tammy, she is amazing, and I would love to have her with me. I'll bring a dish with her for water."

"Good girl, well I'll only be gone for a short while this time, and will lock the downstairs door again."

Beth nodded taking her handkerchief from her pocket to blow her nose. Hart raced off downstairs to see the pharmacist next door.

Mr. Owen lived upstairs over his business with his wife. He closed his doors at five sharp every day, one hour later than Hart. A friendly man with a shiny bald patch and short gray hair surrounding, his bright blue eyes twinkled, and his mouth ever smiled. Thankfully no customers were present, so Hart got quickly to the point.

"Is it true that moonshine is an ingredient in cough medicine Mr. Owen?"

"Indeed it is Mr. Carson, although it's in short supply. Every Pharmacist mixes the formula himself following a recipe. We are supposed to be in for a cold winter snap this year according to the Farmers Almanac. If that's so, then cough medicine will be in short supply." He stopped smiling as this was a severe dilemma for the sick.

"What price is a bottle of moonshine?" Hart's question surprised the other man, yet he felt it was essential to answer.

"Well, buying it wholesale as I do, I pay two dollars a pint, why do you ask?" He looked at Hart strangely. Hart looked right back as he had nothing to hide.

"My secretary is upstairs by herself. If you don't mind, I'll return and talk more about it after I close for the day." He began to walk away.

"Anytime Mr. Carson, I'll be here."

Hart waved his hand in reply and kept walking.

Two clients came in to see him without an appointment after he got back. The second one desired to make his Will, and it was almost time for Hart to close for the day. Sending Beth home, Hart wrote down what the man wanted, then told him to return the next afternoon to sign the original and to take a copy home.

Happy to do this, his client left. Hurriedly Hart locked the Will in his safe before closing up and leaving fifteen minutes late.

The Pharmacist was eagerly waiting for Harts

appearance, quickly serving a customer so that they would leave. He walked to look out on the street, then turning his door plaque to read closed, he locked the door.

"I believe you have good news for me, Mr. Carson, would I be right in my assumption?"

Hart could see the gleam in the man's eyes and wondered how trustworthy he was. Hart decided to test his honesty.

"Yes well, one of my clients has some pint-sized old moonshine for sale. Kept for years, they have decided to sell it for sound production at the right price. They don't want it to get into the wrong hands. Now, if anyone asks me about this, I will know you have talked, and if that happens, then I will advise my client not to sell in these parts."

"Rightly so Mr. Carson, I fully understand. Of course, if you were to sell some to me, I would thankfully pay $4 a pint." He had doubled the amount and rubbed his hands together showing Hart that dollar signs ticked over in his head.

"Yes well, should they sell to you Mr. Owen then you would be the only pharmacist within miles to be able to make up the mixture."

"That's right Sir, and I would be very pleased to do so." He smiled, and for the first time, Hart witnessed a greedy glint.

Hart had no idea what amount of moonshine would go into a bottle for a cough, but since it was 100 percent pure alcohol, he reasoned it was a small quantity.

"How much do you charge customers for this elixir?"

"Why I would need to work that out wouldn't I?"

"Yes well, the people who own this would not like anyone exploited you understand. So if they thought you traded dishonestly, they would sell it to other businesses such as yours."

Mr. Owens face turned bright red. He was about to

retort when he thought better of it. "How many jars can you sell me, Mr. Carson?"

"I believe three dozen, would you be able to use that many?"

"I would indeed Sir, Yes, I believe I would. When can I have them?"

"Sheriff Taylor would keep watch on the sale from afar to make sure of all honesty in the deal. I will need to know when he is available. It would be at around eight o'clock one night this week. They will knock on your back door."

At the mention of the sheriff's name, the pharmacist displayed dismay. "Look here Mr. Carson, why is Sheriff Taylor involved?"

"Only to keep the peace, Mr. Owen, he and his deputies will stand back and make sure that there are no problems. You are safe, and so are the vendors. That's if you still want it?"

"Yes, I assure you that I do Sir, so I am to expect to get a delivery one night this week is that right."

"It is, and cash will exchange for the goods."

The pharmacist looked uneasy but nodded in agreement.

Turning away and letting himself out of the door Hart hoped the sale would run smoothly. He would ask Don to be present because he no longer trusted the friendly Mr. Owen.

*****

Sheriff Taylor decided for Friday night as the pharmacist would be thinking they weren't coming. Don would knock on the door then step back when Mr. Owen answered. It was a good thing he did this as the Owen couple both answered the door with shotguns. They quickly discarded these when they saw the wagon and five other men.

"Sorry Sheriff you can never be too careful at night."

"I hope that's all you were up to Owen. Okay men, unload and we'll get out of here." Don stood back watching with Hart, while Will, Brian and the two deputies soon had the boxes packed into Owen backroom.

Hart received the money, counting it carefully before paying each man except the sheriff five dollars each. The rest was to be locked in Harts office safe until every last jar was gone.

Chapter 25

Plans made.

With still dozens of boxes to be sold, and there had to be an easy way of marketing them. If possible to sell them in one go.

Without experience, Hart had no idea where to begin. He took the problem to his father, but Jeb had no solutions.

Hart would talk it over with Mariah, after all, the moonshine belonged to her, and he knew she would like inclusion.

Sunday afternoon as was their habit, they walked over to sit and talk under the magnolia tree. Hart placed his arm around Mariah's waist holding her close to his left side, and heart. She wore a blue dress today that reflected the color of her eyes, and he knew that she knew, how the color suited her.

Gazing into those lovely eyes now, Hart saw the love

and trust in him reflected.

"My dearest darling, how can I wait until our wedding?" He sighed, "and yet, that's what will make the day so special." He kissed her forehead tenderly.

"I'm at a standstill for how to sell off the remaining cases of alcohol. In selling to our town pharmacist, I have found it not to be as easy as it might look. What to do next? And how to handle it, is a problem."

Mariah's answer surprised him. "My father occasionally had more tobacco than sales for it. What he learned was to advertise around to only those who were reputable buyers." She looked at Hart for his reaction and noting his interest she added. "We want the moonshine to help with cough mixture supplies so why not place an advertisement in the National Community Pharmacists Association magazine?"

"What a great idea my love, you are not only beautiful but clever as well. How did you know of this publication?"

"Well," she smiled cheekily, "Mr. Owen left it on his counter one day, and I picked it up to look through. He took it off me, saying it was for his eyes only." She laughed aloud, "But I got a good look before he did."

"You monkey you!" Hart laughed with her. "Nothing gets hidden from those lovely eyes, does it?"

Turning her face toward his, he kissed her hungrily. "You are so unique, do you know that? Miss. beautiful Mariah."

"Ah, so now you realize it, hey. ALSO, Papa had the buyers come to our dock here in town and sold directly from there."

Hart perked up hearing this. "So money and time are saved, how ingenious, it sounds perfect. I'll get onto Don for the best day and time. We'll need about a month for the news to circulate." Jumping up and pulling Mariah to her feet, he took her hand looping it through his arm, as they walked back to the house.

"I'll get going home to talk to my father again after we

see the cousins, I have complete faith in those two men."

Entering the kitchen Sarah, Fay and Tilly sat at the table drinking tea and talking. Sarah got to her feet bringing two more cups to the table. "We are having our's in peace while the children are upstairs playing hide and seek. They have had milk and cookies," she explained.

"Caleb went off with Will and Brian to pick red raspberries from a full bush they found. We'll make pies and then preserve some if there are plenty." Fay laughed, "they took the wash tub and planned on getting it full."

"I thought they would be out of season in October." Sarah looked baffled.

"No, not this kind and the weather has helped," Hart finished off his tea and got up to leave.

Mariah hadn't finished her's and leaving it got up to see Hart out. Standing together at the open front door, Mariah took her handkerchief out and wiped the sweat from Hart's brow. It was the little demonstrations like this that swelled Hart's love for her. "I'm off then, and will probably come by tomorrow. I love you."

"I love you also," Mariah whispered.

*****

Before opening the office on Monday morning, Hart went to tell Mariah his plans. He would go to the National Community Pharmacists Association at Virginia and personally place the advertisement. "The date is settled for Tuesday evening at five o'clock on the twenty-eighth, Mariah."

Hart looked at her adding, "I leave on the Paddle steamer in an hour and will hopefully be back by Thursday. Pa is filling in at the office for me until then."

"May God go with you bring you back safely, Hart." Mariah kissed him before he hopped into the buggy and took off. She continued to watch until he disappeared from view. When would these problems end, she couldn't wait?

I best go and find Fay to check the catalog for our wedding dress materials.

"Are we finally going to look for our dress material and patterns" Fay got up from sitting on the end of her bed, finishing off the plait in her hair. She found the catalog inside her chest of drawers.

"Let's go and sit out on the front porch in the fresh air," Mariah suggested leading the way. "Oh what a perfect day, neither hot nor cold, just the way I like it."

"Yes," agreed her friend, "same here."

Placing the book between them on a small table, they poured over the beautiful lace patterns.

"What do you prefer Fay? Silk or cotton lace." Mariah looked at her friend who was absorbed in the beauty of colors and patterns.

"Gosh, it's hard as they are all so lovely. It's difficult to know what is silk and what is cotton."

"I think the silk would feel softer, yet the cotton is crisp and might not crease as much."

"Oh Mariah, I believe this light beige is the one for me."

"A good choice as it suits your coloring."

"I'd like to have a lavender blue, but I know my mother would have a fainting spell if I chose that."

"What about a white that has a faint tinge of the blue like this one Mariah, I'm sure she would agree with this."

Mariah studied it carefully. "I think you are right my friend, and my bouquet could be lavender-blue flowers with tiny pink and white ones."

Tommy put his head around the door to give his message. "Tilly said to tell you that breakfast is served and waiting." Before waiting for an answer, he turned and ran back inside calling the dogs after him. "Come on Lucy and Scruffy, I've got a lot of work to do today, and I don't want you slowing me down."

Mariah and Fay heard this and looked at each other to

laugh. "He seriously wants to help to can those berries. I hate to think of the mess he'll get into."

Fay added, "and the stains to his clothes, but it's good that he wants to be a part of the process. It won't be long before little Rebel is doing the same."

"Heaven forbid, I'm glad I'm not Sarah. But," Mariah added, "perhaps I'll have it to look forward to when my children arrive. Anyhow, Fay, we can finish this later, and I'll post off our orders tomorrow."

Chapter 26

True Dreams.

Hart couldn't believe what he heard. The magazine office was prepared to buy the lot, a further one hundred and sixty-two boxes. "Why that's over fifteen thousand dollars at four dollars a bottle, are you sure?"

"Very sure Mr.Carson. The whole U.S. will need as much as we can get this winter. The buyers can pick them up from us, and we will make one dollar a bottle, that is a profitable trade." He turned away to retreat to his desk and write a check for five thousand dollars.

Handing this over to Hart, he informed they would be at Hart's office in one week to complete the trade. "I'll hire a couple of men to ride shotgun in case of trouble, but if we all keep silent about it, there shouldn't be a hitch."

Hart got back early on Thursday and went straight to

inform the sheriff.

"That's fine Hart, and to be on the safe side we'll leave a map to show the directions to Fairways. They will find a party waiting for them in case they try any underhanded stuff." Don gave Hart his no-nonsense look nodding him off as the deputies entered.

Jeb was giving Beth some sound advice about deviate people as Hart walked into his office. He stood up immediately shaking Harts' hand and thumping him on the back. "Glad to see you back, son."

Beth's dog, a Jack Russell growled as a reminder she was there. Hart liked the look of the little pet, knowing this breed stood no nonsense.

Together father and son went into Harts office and closed the door. Keeping his voice low, Hart laid out what was to come about in the following week. Jeb nodded, "I agree to the sheriff being present that's much safer."

*****

Although there was some nervous tension when the wagon arrived at Fairways to collect the goods, they loaded up, paid over the money and left without hardly a word.

A burly looking man drove with a hard-faced male beside him. The third sat atop the canvas that covered the load, protecting from the rear. These men knew what they were doing and were sharp on the job.

Mariah and Hart both breathed a sigh of relief knowing this lot of trouble would relax tension and all would sleep more comfortably.

The tunnel was sealed forever with the only reminder left, the large room at the very end.

Mariah had decided where the money was to go. On Friday night Hart, Caleb, Will, and Brian were invited to supper. Not to leave Tilly in the kitchen to eat alone, Mariah included her.

When the meal finished, Mariah asked Hart, Caleb, Will, and Brian into the sitting room and closed the door. After all were seated Mariah looked at each man, pleased with the genuine goodness all shared.

"I have a little speech and am not sure how to begin. Hart and I have spoken together about a concern to us. Pastor Caleb, you faithfully serve your flock, living on barely enough to feed you. You want to marry, but to do so could mean a long wait."

Mariah observed the pastor looking embarrassed by her words. "Please don't take this the wrong way, Caleb. You are a blessing too many, and with Fay alongside you, it will be a double blessing. We believe the Lord would have us help you."

Bending over from her seat to her receptacle Mariah extracted an envelope. Handing it to the pastor with a smile she quoted a scripture. "God tells us that he will, 'turn our mourning into dancing and our sorrow into joy.' This money came from something wrong, and you will turn it into something right. Fix up the church and make your home fit for a bride."

"What can I say," Caleb spluttered.

Without answering Mariah now turned to the cousins. "Will and Brian, we don't know how we would ever have got by without you two." She looked at Hart who produced a title deed of five acres of land to each man.

They held it in their hands staring at the wording. "It's at the very back of the Plantation off the river road," Brian spoke in amazement to Will.

"So it is," was all that Will could voice.

"Yes, and you will live next door to each other and be able to walk back here to your jobs very easily. BUT wait …. There's more."

Mariah and Hart were enjoying this so much. Seeing the unbelief yet wonder in their eyes was the best reward.

"Mariah picked up two more envelopes. You can both take two weeks vacation and begin to build your houses before the cold weather hits."

She handed the money over. "We are doing this out of selfishness you know so that you will remain with us forever." She chuckled, and Hart joined her.

Will reached over and shook their hands, then Brian followed. "We never in a million year would dream of having our own home this soon."

"No," added Brian, "you have treated us like family from the start, and that's how we think of you. Thank you both, from the bottom of our heart."

Caleb stood up. "Mariah, could you call Fay down, I want to share this with her." His hands trembled as he opened the door allowing her to go before him.

Waiting in the hall, he bound up the stairs to meet his lady as she began to walk down. "The good Lord has provided Fay, through Hart and Mariah. We will have a home, and can now fix the church. I'd say we can marry in a month."

"Oh Caleb, how wonderful." She burst out crying, burying her face against his chest. He patted her back, soothing her with loving words and gently rocking until she calmed. "No more tears now, let's be thankful for the blessing poured on us."

"Oh, I am, I am." Fay looked around for Mariah. "Thank you, Mariah, you didn't have to do this, but you did. Thank you."

Will and Brian got up to leave. "If you don't mind we'll go, a good nights sleep will convince us that this is true and not a dream." They walked off with Brian's arm around Will's shoulder.

"It was good to see the happiness of fulfilled dreams, wasn't it Hart?"

"Yes! It was, but the best happiness is knowing that people love and care about you. Those two cousins will be around for a long time, and as they said, they feel like our family, and they are."

He stood up preparing to call it a night. Their most significant burdens associated with Fairways had disappeared, along with the evil intent by the

Moonshiners. Their mourning now turned into dancing, and their distress into joy.

"It won't be long before your folks arrive and life will settle down to normal. Do we even know the meaning of that word?"

"Normal may be boring, and that will never do Hart. You will be living here; Fay will go to be with Caleb, and new problems will arise, but we'll deal with them together."

"That we will." He kissed her goodnight and left.

Chapter 27

Glad Tidings

Mariah opened her eyes looking towards the window. By tonight she would be Mrs. Hart Carson, a married lady. Closing her eyes again she said a simple prayer thanking God for his help and asking a blessing over her marriage.

"Will I ever return to singing Opera Lord, or will I remain living here. I leave it in your perfect will knowing your plans for us are for good and not for evil. Help me to be a wife who puts her husband first giving him the same respect as unto you. All honor and glory be yours, almighty God and Father, Amen."

Someone was in her room, she sensed it. There was no sound of entry so who could it be? Slowly her eyes re-opened, and there he was, the magnificent angel from her first night in this house.

"Peace be with you Mariah, and to all who live under this roof. Faithful servant, you have done the Will of God

in how you handled your given task. Rejoice in the Lord always, pray and let your partitions be known, and he will hear. Never allow the SPIRIT of FEAR entry into your heart, you are a child of the King and most worth, of Power, Love, and a sound mind. Although you won't see me, I will always be near; I bid you Farewell."

"Farewell, Gods messenger. I will never forget you or your words."

Throwing back the bedcovers and feet on the floor, Mariah wandered to the window and looked out. A weak sun shone on what seemed a chilly day. Her mantle clock rang out six tiny chimes, only seven hours away from her wedding. Her lovely gown hung on the wardrobe door waiting for the time to adorn her as a bride. Today was the day she and Hart had long anticipated. They're joining together as one, in spirit and soul.

Tapping on Mariah's closed door, it opened a crack for her mother's head to peep around and see if she were awake. "I thought you'd be up, did you sleep at all?"

She entered the room sparkling with happiness.

"I did, thank you Momma, but I'm well awake now and unsure what to do first."

"I don't blame you, yet there are still hours to go, that's why I came to help." Her mother walked to the door, "how about I put on the water to heat for your bath, then you can come to breakfast in a housecoat and keep it on for your hair styling."

"That's a beautiful idea; I'll collect the new undergarments you bought for me in Paris, and tidy up this room. My bath will probably be ready by then."

Singing to herself, with a dance in her step Mariah tidied her bed then lay the gown out on the cover. Thankfully she didn't need to go out into the cold air and was glad they had chosen not to marry at the church, or she would have frozen without a coat.

Everything was cheery at the breakfast table with Mariah's father entertaining with funny stories of getting language confused in Peking. "I tried sign language and finally, our guide understood. Then in Venice, your mother got into the wrong gondola and not knowing I was with her, the gondolier took off. I had to pay to follow her in another one. I kept shouting for him to stop, but they couldn't hear me."

Both parents laughed while relating how funny they must have looked to other tourists. Their stories made Mariah relax and feel at ease. Thinking back on it later, she realized this was what they intended, and loved them so much for doing it.

Fay fashioned Mariah's hair in a plated coronet with stray wisps of hair loose on either side of her face. She looked stunning when the wedding gown came down over her head to be buttoned up all down the back. It clung to her curves pulling in at the waist.

Once Mariah was ready her mother and Fay rushed downstairs to take their seats, nodding to the lady who was to play the piano. Hart stood up front with Caleb anxiously waiting and fidgeting with his necktie.

John Kingsford stood at the top of the stairs, waiting to escort his daughter below. Music flowed for the wedding march as they came down the stairs and entered the sitting room. Hart caught his breath at the sight of his bride; she was beyond his expectation for a wife, and he counted himself honored to become her husband.

Tommy and Rebel sat up front not to miss anything. While Caleb performed the marriage service, Mariah faintly heard the young Tommy question his mother as to when she would get married. With Will seated beside her, Sarah turned red with embarrassment. Will thought is wonderful for Tommy to speak out, as he cared for Sarah and the children very much.

Jeb's housekeeper helped with the cooking and serving the food. Milly seemed younger than her age with her new found happiness. Jeb waltzed with her when the time came, but the crowed floor soon made it impossible. A photographer brought in for the occasion took the newlyweds into the hall for photos. It was far too cold to venture outside.

"Looks like winter is hitting early this year Jeb commented. We are going home before that wind whips up stronger." Rugging up in coats, hats, and scarf, and into the buggy with extra blankets and taking the housekeeper they hurried away.

By four o'clock the wind howled making a terrible noise. "Honey I don't believe it safe to venture out in this weather, dad was right in going an hour ago, but it's too risky now."

The photographer had left straight after Jeb so he should be safe. Caleb would remain for the night which he didn't mind. It the weather stayed as terrible as it was, there would be no church tomorrow.

Calling Sarah to help, she and Fay went upstairs to prepare Mariah's room for the newly married. "Let's make it as romantic as we can Sarah. If you can help me change the bed with fresh sheets, then I'll go and collect a tray of tit-bits for nibbling later."

Fay pulled out a new quilt for the top of the bed, and it dressed it to perfection. With all done, Fay began to leave the room when she remembered the fire needed lighting.

"Can you ask Will and Brian to bring up wood for the bedroom fire and light it, Sarah, after that, we are finished."

Sarah returned to Mariah's bedroom with the men. Brian went straight back to the wedding party, but Will took his time to lay and light the fire.

"Its cozy isn't it Sarah? Did you know that Brian and I each own five acres of land and we have the money to build a house each?"

"I heard a rumor to that effect," Sarah admitted.

"I'll be looking for a wife then," Will looked her in the eye. Sarah said nothing which didn't make it easy for him. Knowing the need to talk straight, he stood up from the now roaring fire.

"I care for you and the children Sarah, do you suppose I could court you once I build the house?" He smiled in his typically gentle fashion, and Sarah melted.

"Yes, Will, I believe that would be nice. Thank you for considering the children and me."

"You are a bonnie woman; I couldn't ask for better."

He caught her hand, then kissed her cheek. "Let's go down and let them know the room is ready; I'm sure the newlyweds will be happy to hear it."

Epilogue

Swansborough 1907

The thirteen-year-old Tommy raced after Will begging to be able to help with the plowing. "I can do it Pa, I'm almost as tall as you, and I won't get tired."

"Next year," Will answered. "Your mother needs help, and Rebel will be able to give some by then." Seeing Tommy was preparing to argue Will stopped him before he began. "Womenfolk are not as strong as us, son, and you remember that. She has your two little brothers to care for as well as us and needs your hand." He rustled Tommy's hair, "but I appreciate you asking."

Whistling Lucy, Tommy returned to the house knowing his father relied on him, and this was a responsibility that Tommy took seriously. If his father knew he was trustworthy with this, then he would have confidence in him for the plow next year.

Brian had recently married a young woman from across the valley. Both worked at the plantation home for

Mariah and Hart. Brian's wife Gracey helped with the cooking and washing. While her mother Mary acted as housekeeper, and father Len worked the orchard. None of the work was hard; the wage was reasonable, and each worked four days a week.

Hart worked five days at his office and was busy with newcomers moving to the area. On Saturday he helped with outside plantation work and Sunday was a rest day for all.

He and Mariah had two children of their own, a girl Charity aged four and a son Aiden just turned one year. Fairways plantation was now an apple orchard including a few dozen peach trees for bee pollination. This year was their first for fruit picking, and the trees were loaded, promising a good harvest.

Everyone would be involved in getting the crop picked, and if the demand became favorable, Hart considered taking an apprentice straight out of college to help run his law office.

He decided he belonged to the outdoor life close to his family. His office helper could take over the majority of the legalities as he became proficient. Hart smiled to himself as he thought about this, he enjoyed working in the fresh air.

Jeb and Milly often visited Fairways and took Charity back home with them on occasion. They loved the little ones, who brought out the mothering instinct in Milly. Mariah appreciated having some occasional free time as she suspected she was pregnant again and often felt sleepy.

She wondered what this baby would be, boy or girl, either way, it didn't matter, but her hands certainly would be full.

Twice a year she gave a concert in the new church hall. Always well attended it kept her voice preserved. Singing to her was as familiar as breathing. She sang all day long bringing happiness to all who enjoyed hearing her.

Caleb with Fay had a boy of their own. There would be no more for them after Fay's difficult birth. Lucas was three years old and full of energy. He resembled his father with strawberry blond hair, but his eyes were his mothers. Caleb joked and said his son got the best of both parents.

Fay was active in the church leading Bible study once a week. So far there were many baptized in the local river. Whenever this happened, the whole church celebrated with a picnic. Due to the church encouraging socializing the community were closer and helped each other much more than before.

Tilly still worked for Mariah and saved her wages. She could read and write as well as anyone now and received tutoring by Miss. Hogan after school hours learning to type. Hart knew his secretary Beth would need a helper before long and Tilly was first in line for the job.

At the sound of working in a law office, Tilly's chest puffed out with pride. She knew what she wanted in life now, all due to her faith in the risen Lord.

The End

Please Post a Review

If you enjoyed reading House of Shadows, Secrets never Die, then I pray that you will take the time to share your thoughts about this story and write a review. So many books are on the market, and Christian Books need to stand out as a witness to our faith. With this in mind, every review written helps the author to continue writing.

Reviews don't need to be perfect.

They don't need to be lengthy.

They are a welcome contribution from you, to me.

So please write a few words and nominate how many STARS the book deserves.

May the Lord Bless you and keep you under cover of his wings.

Crystal Mary Lindsey (Bible College Graduate).

Other Christian Fiction Books by this author are:

Cherished Encounter – Romance, Supernatural, Medical, Mystery.

Discovering Treasure – Historical Romance (the 1920s) Mystery, Fun. #1

Forbidden Fruit Temptation – Historical Romance (the 1950s) Mystery, Supernatural, Medical.

Consuming Fire – Contemporary, Romance, Medical. Humor.

Love's Time – Historical Romance (the 1920s) Supernatural,

Spirit Warrior – Historical Romance (the 1920's), Supernatural,

Yasmin finds THE WAY – Contemporary Romance, Mystery. Medical.

The Mystery Healer of Smoky Mountain – Historical Romance, Mystery. Medical,

CHRISTIAN NON FICTION

Abuse Beaten From Victim to Victor   A True story
with self-help.   (I wrote the story about my
abuse to help others)

Sure Fire Self-Help and Knowledge of Health Care (I am
a retired R.N. B.S.N. M.H.N. Prof C.) Having specialised
in Emergency Medicine and Mental Health.

Lightning Source UK Ltd.
Milton Keynes UK
UKHW040740010219
336544UK00001B/98/P